Angel Food for Boys & Girls
Volume II

Angel Food
for
Boys & Girls

Volume II

"Angel Food Time"
Little Talks to Young Folks

Father Gerald T. Brennan

Neumann Press
Gastonia, North Carolina

Nihil Obstat:
        Benedict A. Ehmann
                Censor Deputatus

Imprimatur:
        ✠ James E. Kearney
                Bishop of Rochester

March 3, 1953

ISBN 978-0-911845-67-9

Printed and bound in the United States of America.

Neumann Press
Gastonia, North Carolina
www.TANBooks.com

2013

Contents

Angel Food
for
Boys & Girls

Volume II

1. The Boy
Who Weighed an Elephant

MANY years ago the people of India wanted to show their Prince that they really loved him. So they gave their Prince a strange gift. You'll never guess what the people gave the Prince, so I might as well tell you. The people of India gave their Prince a white elephant.

Now you must know that in India the size of a gift tells the person who receives it how much he is loved. So, when the Prince saw the white elephant, he was very happy, but he was curious, too. He wanted to know just how much his people loved him. So the Prince decided to have the elephant weighed. And that's where the Prince ran into trouble.

Do you know that there were no scales in all India large enough or strong enough to hold the mighty elephant? But that didn't stop the Prince. The Prince was determined that he would find out just how much his people loved him. The Prince was determined to have his elephant weighed. In fact, the

Prince offered a reward for anyone who could weigh his white elephant.

Several people tried to weigh the elephant and several others had ideas as to how it should be done, but all these people failed. Then one day a little boy went to the Prince, and the little fellow told the Prince that he would weigh the white elephant. The Prince smiled at the boy and some friends of the Prince even laughed. Imagine a little boy trying to do something that no one else could do! Imagine a little boy weighing an elephant!

The Prince, however, decided to give the boy a chance. He wondered what the boy would do. How would the little fellow weigh the white elephant?

It seems that the boy's father owned a large flat-bottomed boat on the river. Oh, it was a very, very large boat, and the boy led the white elephant onto the boat. Of course, just as soon as the elephant was on the boat, the boat sank very low in the water. Then the boy painted a black line around the sides of the boat showing how deep the boat had sunk into the water while the elephant was on board. After that, the boy led the elephant off the boat. Just as soon as the elephant was off the boat, the boat rose up in the water.

Then the boy carried stones from the shore and placed the stones in the boat. For weeks the boy carried stones and, as he placed more stones in the boat, the boat sank deeper into the water. Finally, the boat sank down to the black line the boy had painted around the sides of the boat when the elephant had been on it. When the boy saw his black line touch the water, he was very happy. Now half of his work was done.

The boy still had a big job to do. Can you guess what the boy did then? The boy weighed each stone on that boat. Oh, it took the little fellow a long, long time to weigh all those stones, but when he had finished weighing the stones, he knew just how much the white elephant weighed. The stones pushed the big boat down into the water to the black line just as the elephant had pushed the boat down into the water to the black line. So now the weight of the stones was the exact weight of the white elephant.

When the little boy told the Prince how much the elephant weighed, the Prince was pleased. The Prince knew then how much his people loved him, and the Prince knew, too, that the little boy who weighed his white elephant was a very clever little fellow.

I suppose you are wondering whether the Prince rewarded the boy. Yes, the Prince kept his word. He gave the boy a black and white pony as a reward, and the little fellow felt that his black and white pony was a mighty fine reward for weighing a white elephant.

Children, your life weighs up or is equal to all the little things you think, say, and do. Your life weighs up to all your thoughts, words, and actions. Every thought, every word, every action of yours puts a stone on your boat of life. If your thoughts, words, and actions are good, then you will carry a good load through life. If your thoughts, words, and actions are bad, then you will carry a bad load through life. When you die, God will weigh every thought, word, and action. If your thoughts, words, and actions have been good, God will reward you. If your thoughts, words, and actions have been bad, God will punish you.

Yes, there will be a weighing time for everyone of you. You will stand before God and God will be just. His scales won't tell any lies. It will be too late then to correct any mistakes. It will be too late then to ask for another chance. You have only one chance to save your soul and that chance is right now. If your thoughts, words, and actions are good now, you won't have to worry when you stand before God.

The little boy in our story found how much the elephant weighed by adding up a lot of little stones. God will do the same thing. God will weigh up every little thought, word, and action to see whether you deserve heaven. So, keep your thoughts clean! Keep your speech clean! Do good every chance you get! Fill your boat of life with everything that is good. That's the way to get to heaven.

God bless you and take good care of yourself!

2. The Orphan's Plea

SEVERAL months ago I visited a home for orphans in the great city of Havana. It was a beautiful place, a grand home where one thousand children lived together, played together, and went to school together. Some of the children had no father. Some had no mother. Others had no parents at all. Yet, the children were not sad children. Oh, no! Most of the children seemed to be very happy.

One of the good Sisters showed me the many buildings. I saw the chapel where the children went to Mass. I saw the dining rooms where they ate their meals. I saw the children's hospital, their game rooms, and their playground. Then the Sister asked me to visit the school. Well, I visited every room in that school and had a grand time. The children sang Spanish songs and some English songs, too. They recited pieces. Some of the children even posed for a picture.

Now I must tell you about the last room I visited. It was one of several kindergartens in that school. When I entered the room, I found about thirty little children and they were all very busy. Some were playing with blocks, and others were making funny animals out of colored clay. A few boys were coloring pictures and some of the girls were making mats for the table. Most of the children smiled and went right along with their work. They were too busy to pay much attention to me. But there was one little fellow sitting in the corner who stopped his work and looked at me. This little boy was about five years old and he smiled very easily. When I smiled at him, he smiled right back. Then, all of a sudden, what do you think happened?

The little boy left his place in the corner, hurried to the front of the room, and stood right in front of me. I looked down at the little fellow, but I didn't say anything. Finally, the little boy pulled on my coat. "Father," he asked, "will you lift me up?"

I suppose you are wondering whether I lifted up the little fellow. You bet I lifted him up, and I held him in my arms for some time. That little boy wanted to be noticed. That little boy wanted to be loved.

I have thought about that little boy in Havana many, many times, and I have thought, too, about his strange request. "Father, will you lift me up?" Oh, I wish that you children would remember those words, and I wish that you would say them often to God: "Father, will You lift me up?"

I know that you boys and girls want to save your souls. I know that you are trying to save your souls. That's why you pray. That's why you go to Mass. That's why you go to confession and receive Holy

Communion. You want to be near God. You want to be near your Father. I know that every time you go to confession you promise God that you will never sin again. But what happens? When you are not on guard, the devil tempts you and leads you into sin. When you fall into sin, children, don't give up! Call upon God, your Father, right away, and ask God to lift you up! Ask God to forgive you!

You know, children, that God, your Father, is very kind. He is always ready to forgive you, but you must be sorry. No matter how many times you fall into sin, God is always ready to lift you up, but you must ask Him to lift you up, and you must be sorry. God never refuses to lift up a sinner. God loves sinners when they are sorry.

Don't ever get the idea that God doesn't love you! Don't ever get the idea that you have hurt God too much to be forgiven! If you fall into sin, go to confession and tell God you are sorry! Remember, God loves you most when He hears you say, "Father, will You lift me up?"

God bless you and take good care of yourself!

3. A Little Girl's Prayer

GOD must like little Killeen Farrell very much. Killeen, you know, is eight years old and in the third grade at Saint Monica's school. Like all little girls, Killeen likes to play, but she likes to work, too. The little girl helps her mother with the dishes, dusts her room, and runs errands. Most of the day Killeen is a very busy girl, but no matter how busy she is, Killeen Farrell always has time for God.

Now, I know that all little children are tired at night. After they have worked and played all day, little boys and girls are very tired. That's why little children go to bed early. Of course, little Killeen Farrell is tired at night, too, but tired or not, Killeen always says her prayers.

When Killeen says her prayers at night, her older brother, Billy, prays with her, too. The children take turns saying the prayers. One night Killeen says the prayers and Billy answers her. Then the next night Billy says the prayers and Killeen answers. Of course, the children's mother also prays with them, but the other night Mrs. Farrell was busy in the next room. The mother heard something that pleased her very much, something that made her smile.

It was Killeen's turn to say the night prayers. The little girl said the usual prayers and, when she finished, she didn't make the Sign of the Cross. The little girl stayed on her knees and made up a prayer of her own. Looking up at the crucifix that hung over the bed, little Killeen prayed like this: "God bless Mommy and keep her well! Take good care of Dad and help him to sell more stoves!" Then the little girl stopped for a moment and finally finished her prayer. "Take good care of Yourself, God," she said, "because if anything ever happened to You, we'd sure be up against it."

Children, I'm quite sure that all of you feel just like little Killeen Farrell. You know that you need God. You know that God watches over you every minute of the day and night and you want God to keep watching over you. You want God to help you and take care of you. You know that God is good to you. He lets you live and gives you your parents, your happiness, your health, and your friends. God gives you fresh air, sunshine, and rain. He gives you food to eat and water to drink. Oh, God gives you so many things that you can't name all of them. Why, you need God so much that you couldn't get along without Him.

Sometime you may meet a person who will tell you that he doesn't need God. That person may tell you that he can live without God. But he is only fooling himself. I met a man once who told me that he was living without God and that he didn't need

God. But then, what happened? One day that man became very sick and he sent for me. The man begged me to pray for him. He begged me to teach him how to pray so that he could ask God's help. The man knew that no doctor could help him. The man found out that he needed God.

It's a good thing to know that God is taking care of you. If God were not around, you would find it very hard to be good. You know how many times a day the devil bothers you and tries to lead you into sin. Doesn't God always tell you to chase the devil away? Certainly, He does! You need God at all times, You need God very much.

You know how much your daddy does for you. You know that your daddy works hard so that you can have a good home, warm clothes to wear, and food to eat. Your daddy wants you to be happy because he loves you. Now wouldn't it be terrible if you had no daddy? Yes, it would be very, very hard. Well, don't forget that God is your Father, too! God loves you even more than your own daddy loves you, and God does bigger things for you. So, you need God. You need God to watch over you. You need God to protect you. You need God to take care of you.

Ask God, then, to take good care of you, and tell God to take good care of Himself, because if anything ever happened to Him, we'd sure be up against it!

God bless you and take good care of yourself!

4. The Devil at Coney Island

ONE day last summer the devil was tired of working and decided to take a day's vacation. He knew that his many helpers would work hard while he enjoyed a holiday. And where do you think the devil went? He went to Coney Island. Coney Island, you know, is a large amusement park near Brooklyn, and the park stretches along the shore of the Atlantic Ocean.

You can imagine how much fun the devil had at Coney Island. He rode on the roller coaster and the merry-go-round. He went to the shooting gallery and shot clay pigeons and ducks. He threw baseballs at a funny clown and won cigarettes. He had his picture taken and even sent post cards to some of his friends in hell. Of course, the devil feasted on hot dogs, Coca-Cola, and ice cream. Oh, the devil had a grand time on his holiday at Coney Island and he enjoyed every minute of it.

During the afternoon the devil lay on the sand for a long time and rested. Yes, he even fell asleep and enjoyed a grand nap. When the devil awoke, what do you suppose he decided to do? He decided

to go bathing. Yes, the devil went bathing in the Atlantic Ocean.

Now, the devil couldn't swim. So at first, the devil was very careful. Little by little, however, he walked into deeper water. Little by little, he walked farther away from the shore. Well, the devil walked out a little bit too far, and, all of a sudden, the devil was in trouble. The waves dashed up over the devil's head and he began to sink.

"Help! Save me! I'm drowning!" cried out the devil at the top of his voice.

Three boys, Francis, Tom, and Terry Robarge, heard the devil's cries. The boys were all good swimmers and they swam toward the devil as fast as they could. Sure enough, the three brothers saved the devil's life.

When the devil and the boys reached the shore, the devil thanked the brothers for saving his life. "Now," said the devil, "I'm going to reward you. I'm going to give each one of you whatever you want."

"What do you want for a reward?" the devil asked Francis Robarge.

"I want a new bicycle," answered Francis quickly.

"Well, I'll see that you get a new bicycle," smiled the devil as he shook the boy's hand.

Turning to Tom the devil asked the same question. "What do you want for a reward?"

Tom thought for a moment and then answered the devil's question. Tom wanted a fishing rod and a reel. Then and there, the devil promised to get Tom a fishing rod and a reel.

Of course, the devil wondered what the third brother wanted. And was the devil surprised! What do you think Terry wanted? Terry Robarge wanted a nice funeral.

"A nice funeral!" gasped the devil in surprise. "That's a strange request for a little boy. Why do you want a nice funeral?"

"I want a nice funeral," answered Terry, "because I know that, when I go home and tell my father that I saved the devil's life, my father is going to kill me."

Now, children, that's only a story, but I think that the idea behind the story is a very good one. I'm quite sure that Terry's father wouldn't kill him because the boy saved the devil's life, but it shows how his father felt toward the devil. The father hated the devil and he would have been very happy if the devil had drowned. Terry's father knew all the trouble the devil has caused in this world. He knew the thousands of people the devil has led into sin. He knew how many times the devil has hurt God. No wonder Terry's father hated the devil!

Children, you, too, should feel the same way toward the devil. You should hate him. You should keep away from him. Remember, the devil is God's biggest enemy. The devil is your greatest enemy. Ever since God punished the devil by sending him to hell, the devil has been working against God. He has been trying to steal souls from God. That's why the devil, at times, tries to be nice to you. He makes sin look nice. He tempts you and tries to lead you into sin. The devil wants to steal your soul from God.

If you ever get into trouble, the devil won't save your life and he won't save your soul, either. In fact, the devil wants you to lose your life of happiness with God. The devil wants you to lose your soul. So, don't ever get chummy with the devil! Keep away from him, because he's a bad actor and he'll do harm to you every chance he gets! Let the devil go to Coney Island or any other place, but you keep away from him!

God bless you and take good care of yourself!

5. The Boy
Who Dusted the Devil's Tail

EUGENE NEWSOME was my idea of a first-class altar boy. In fact, he was the best altar boy who served Mass in old Saint Charles Church. The little fellow was always on time, always neat and clean, and very serious. Serving Mass was never a job for little Eugene. It was a privilege. It was an honor for him to help the priest at the altar.

All the priests and Sisters at Saint Charles liked Eugene. They liked him because he was always so willing to help. That's why Sister Clement, who had charge of the altar, often asked Eugene to help her with her work. Every Saturday morning Eugene was on the job to help Sister Clement. He helped with the candles. He helped with the flowers. He polished candlesticks, filled the holy-water fonts, and kept the altar boys' robes in perfect order. You can see, then, that Eugene was Sister Clement's right-hand man.

Well, one Saturday Eugene had worked very hard all morning. He was tired and decided to go home.

"Is there anything else you want me to do?" he asked Sister Clement.

"Yes!" answered Sister quickly. "Will you dust Saint Michael's statue before you go?"

Eugene nodded his head, took a cloth and a chair, and started for the statue. For a moment he stood before the statue and smiled. Saint Michael, you know, was Eugene's hero. The boy liked Saint Michael because he stood there so bravely sticking his spear right through the devil. Eugene liked Saint Michael so much that he felt like shaking the Saint's hand, but he knew he couldn't do that because he was in church.

Eugene stood on the chair and began to dust. He dusted high and he dusted low. The little fellow gave Saint Michael the best dusting he ever had. After all, wasn't Saint Michael the boy's hero? Sure, he was, and Eugene wanted Saint Michael to look his very best for the people who would see him the next morning.

Finally, Eugene sat down on the chair. Boy, he was tired, but he still had work to do. He still had to dust the devil's tail. Well, that was one job that the little fellow didn't like. So he wasn't too particular. After all, the devil was a bad fellow and why should the boy try to make him look nice? He stroked the devil's tail twice with his cloth and suddenly stopped. His dust cloth fell to the floor and Eugene Newsome fell sound asleep.

"Eugene!" called a voice in his sleep and the little

fellow raised his head. And what do you think? There standing before the boy was the devil. Yes, it was the devil from hell all dressed in red with a very long tail.

"Eugene," said the devil, "I have come to thank you for dusting my tail and to reward you. Come with me and I'll give you a grand present!"

The little fellow could hardly believe his eyes or his ears. Yes, it was the devil all right and he seemed very friendly. The devil was trying to be kind, and little Eugene believed in him.

Well, the devil walked and walked and little Eugene followed him. They walked in places where Eugene had never been before, and all the time the devil did most of the talking.

"Maybe the devil isn't such a bad fellow after all," thought Eugene to himself several times. The devil certainly wasn't mean or nasty like so many people had said he is. Eugene began to change his mind about the old fellow. No, the devil was not bad at all. He was a kind fellow, very friendly, and certainly very good to Eugene.

Eugene and the devil walked a long time and, finally, they came to a river. It wasn't a very wide river and the water was very clear. "Here we are!" said the devil as he smiled down on the little boy.

For a moment, Eugene was afraid. He wondered what the devil would do next. He almost wished that he hadn't come. He knew then that he was taking a big chance going to a strange place with the big devil himself. Oh, there were so many ways that the devil could have harmed the little boy. No wonder Eugene was afraid!

Of course, the devil didn't know what little Eugene was thinking and, maybe, it was just as well that he didn't know. The big fellow stood looking across the river for some time. Then he spoke very kindly.

"You will find three bags of gold on the other side of the river," said the devil to the boy. "Go over there and take all you want as a reward for dusting my tail!"

Little Eugene's eyes snapped when he heard the words. Immediately, he dove into the water and swam across the river to the other side. And sure enough, at the foot of a tree the little boy found three white bags. When he opened the bags, he could hardly believe his eyes. Yes, the three bags were filled with gold.

Well, it didn't take Eugene very long to fill all his pockets with gold. He even filled his shirt with gold and also slipped some of the gold into his shoes. Now the gold was heavy, and the boy took so much of it that he could hardly walk.

Then Eugene jumped into the water again and tried to swim. Oh, but the boy couldn't swim. He had too much gold and the gold weighed him down so much that he began to sink. He tried to save himself but he was helpless. The devil's gold was dragging the boy down to the bottom of the river. Finally, the boy made one strong try. He fought with all his might to get to the top of the water. He swung his arms and fought so hard that, suddenly, the boy awoke. For a moment, he was afraid. Then he realized that it was all a dream.

Let me tell you that Eugene did no more dusting that day. And as the little boy walked slowly home he muttered to himself: "Gee, I almost lost my life just because I dusted the devil's tail."

That day Eugene Newsome learned a very valuable lesson, and I hope that you, too, will learn the same lesson. Don't ever do any favors for the devil! Remember, he's a sly, foxy fellow, and he'll lead you into trouble every chance he gets. He may pretend to be your friend but don't forget that he hates you. So be on your guard! The devil's gifts will get you into trouble every time. *Children, never trust the devil!*

God bless you and take good care of yourself!

6. Eggs

EASTER SUNDAY, the day Jesus rose from the dead, is also known as egg day. That's the day when boys and girls search the house for nests of eggs, and it is also the day when children eat many eggs. Well, last Easter I found a nest of colored eggs right on my dining-room table. In the center of the nest sat a white Easter rabbit and all around the rabbit lay colored eggs. One egg was green and another was pink. There was a brown egg, a yellow egg, and two purple eggs. Of course, I smiled when I saw the bunny and the eggs, and the rabbit seemed to smile right back at me.

I watched the bunny and eggs in my Easter nest during several meals and then I decided to eat one of the eggs. All of the eggs looked so bright and colorful that I didn't know which egg to choose. Finally, I decided to try the yellow egg. I broke the shell very carefully and ate the egg. Yes, children, that yellow egg was a very good egg.

The next day I decided to have another egg. The green egg was a beautiful looking egg and I decided to try that one. I removed the green shell very carefully and took one bite of the egg. Ugh! The egg was bad. I couldn't eat that green egg and had to throw it away. Then and there I thought that *a beautiful shell certainly doesn't make a good egg*.

When you break the shell of an egg, you never know what you will find inside. You may find a good egg inside and you may find a bad one. In other words, you can't tell an egg from the shell. Now it's the same with boys and girls. I can't tell whether you are good or bad just by looking at you. It's what is inside of you that counts; it's your soul.

Isn't it true that very often you hear some of your friends called "good eggs" and "bad eggs"? When people talk like that, they mean that their souls are either good or bad. When a boy treats you to half of his candy bar, you know that the boy is kind and has a good soul and you say that he is a good egg. The boy who obeys is a good egg. The friend who takes you fishing is a good egg. The mailman, the policeman, the fireman, the nurse in school, they are always doing good and they are all good eggs. Why, you know any number of good eggs, and you know many bad eggs, too. The fellow who steals your bike is a bad egg. The girl who tells lies about you is a bad egg. Whoever ties your clothes in knots while you are swimming is a bad egg. In other words, people who do right and act right and have good souls are good eggs. People who do wrong are bad eggs.

You are either a good egg or a bad one. It all depends on your soul. If your soul is clean, if you always try to obey God's laws, if you say your prayers and receive Holy Communion often, if you go to Mass every Sunday, then you are a good egg. On the other hand, if your soul is dirty with sin, if you break God's laws, if you lie, steal, or cheat, if you disobey, if you keep away from God, then you are a bad egg. Oh, you may wear fine clothes, but don't forget that your looks don't count very much. It's what is inside of you that matters. Your soul is the thing that makes you either a good egg or a bad egg.

Can a bad egg become a good egg? Certainly! You have heard about Mary Magdalene many times. People said that Mary was a bad egg because she lived in sin. Then one day Mary went to Jesus and told Him that she was sorry for her sins. Did Jesus turn Mary away? He did not. Jesus forgave Mary because she was sorry, and Mary Magdalene turned from a bad egg into a good egg. Mary Magdalene became a saint.

When Jesus hung on the cross, a thief hung on a cross next to Him. The thief knew he was a bad egg and he begged Jesus to forgive him his sins. Did Jesus listen to the thief? Certainly, He did! Jesus forgave the dying thief and the thief died without sins. The thief died a good egg.

Oh, I could tell you about many others who were bad eggs for a time. But Jesus forgave those sinners when they were sorry. Jesus turned bad eggs into good eggs. Jesus taught that all bad eggs can become good eggs.

Now you may think that you are a bad egg this morning because you have sins on your soul. You may feel that you have so many sins that Jesus won't forgive you. If you feel that way, you are wrong. No matter how many sins you have, they can all be forgiven. All that you have to do is go to Jesus and tell Him that you are sorry. Jesus will forgive you because He wants your soul to be clean. Jesus wants you to be a good egg.

Then, too, you may know some boy or girl who has been away from Jesus for a long time. You may know someone who is really a bad egg. Why don't you speak to that person and tell him that Jesus will forgive him? In this way you can help some bad egg to become a good egg.

Children, the important part of you is your soul. Your soul is more important than your body. So take good care of your soul! Keep your soul clean! Remember, the colored shell doesn't make a good Easter egg, and fine clothes don't make you a good boy or a good girl. It's your soul that is important. *It's what is inside that counts.*

God bless you and take good care of yourself!

7. Buttons

THIS morning I want to talk about buttons. Yes, I want to say a word about those tiny things that are so important and so helpful. You all wear buttons. You all need buttons. You have buttons on your shirts, buttons on your blouses, and buttons on your coats. There are white buttons, black buttons, red buttons, blue buttons. There are all kinds of buttons that you wear every day. And believe me, those buttons are very important.

Did you ever notice how closely a button clings to a shirt or coat the first time you wear the garment? Yes, that's true! But then what happens? If you wear the coat or shirt often, the button slowly becomes loose and, day by day, the button gets farther away from the cloth. Now if you don't tighten the button with new thread, what happens? You know what happens. You lose your button. So, whenever a button gets loose, be sure and have your mother tighten the button with new thread! Buttons must be kept close to your shirt or coat. Keep the thread tight and then you will never have any trouble with your buttons.

When you were baptized, children, your soul was very close to God. But what has happened? I dare say that your soul doesn't cling so closely to God this morning. And why? Because down through the years time and time again you have fallen into venial sin, and every venial sin has pulled you a little away from God. This morning I'd like to warn you. If you keep on committing venial sins, if you keep on pulling your soul away from God, some day you may fall into a mortal sin. Then your soul would be cut off entirely from God, and you certainly don't want that to happen.

Children, every sin is an offense against God. Every sin hurts God. Even a venial sin hurts God. Sometimes boys and girls think that God doesn't mind venial sins. "A venial sin is only a small sin," they say, "and God doesn't care." Well, God does care. God doesn't like any sin, even the smallest one, because He knows that every little sin draws you away from Him. God hates sin and He wants you to hate sin.

The devil, you know, is always on the job. He is always working against God. He is always working for your soul. Now, the devil doesn't try to pull you away from God suddenly. He takes his time and works slowly. The devil starts off with little things. First, he tries to get you to like sin by tempting you to do something small against God. When you obey him and commit your first venial sin, the devil smiles and waits for another chance. Then, the devil tempts you again to commit another venial sin and then another and another. He gets you used to committing venial sins. Then, when he is sure that you like sin and that you are not afraid of God, the devil tempts you into mortal sin. Can't you see, then, how each venial sin draws you farther away from God? Each venial sin hurts you. Don't forget it!

So don't get the idea that venial sins are not important! They are very important. Venial sins do much harm, much damage, even though you call them small sins.

When you have a loose button on your coat or shirt, what do you usually do? Well, I know what you should do. Just as soon as you see that a button is loose, you should ask your mother to tighten the button. The button belongs close to your shirt or coat. Now if your soul has slipped away from God because of your venial sins, then you should do everything that will help you keep away from those small sins because your soul belongs close to God. You should pray and you should pray, especially, when the devil tempts you. You should go to confession often and receive our Lord often in Holy Communion. You should keep away from the persons, places, and things that lead you into sin.

When you are sick, you go to the doctor. Even though you are not very sick, you take the doctor's medicine because you want to be well again. If you will do the simple things that I've told you to do, you will cure yourself of all venial sins. Why don't you take one venial sin at a time? Avoid that one sin every day and make sure that you don't commit it! Then, when you are very sure that you are not committing that sin any more, take another venial sin and work on that one! If you do that, you'll find that in a very short time you'll not be committing any venial sins at all. In other words, you'll be living the life of a saint and your soul will be just where it belongs — very close to God.

Children, take a good look at your buttons, the buttons on your shirts and the buttons on your coats! Are you sure you're not losing any buttons? Be sure that your buttons cling close to your shirts and coats at all times! And every time you look at a tiny button, think of your soul! Make sure at all times that your soul is not slipping away from God by your venial sins! Keep away from every small sin and your soul will cling to God. That's where your soul belongs!

God bless you and take good care of yourself!

8. Toby Goes to a Party

TOBY PARKER was excited. Toby had been invited to a Halloween party and the little girl knew that the party would be lots of fun. What would she wear? That was the first thought that came to Toby's mind. Should she dress like a gypsy or a Spanish lady? Should she be Snow White or Little Red Riding Hood? Maybe she should dress like a boy. Well, Toby thought and thought, and, finally, what do you suppose Toby decided to wear?

"Guess I'll be a devil," said Toby to her mother, "and I'll scare everybody."

"Oh, no, you won't be a devil," answered the mother. "Devils are bad, and you don't want to be bad. Besides, who ever saw a girl devil?"

"Aren't girls ever devils?" asked Toby very seriously.

Toby's mother laughed. She felt that there must be some girl devils in hell. So the mother agreed to let Toby dress like a devil.

Now, several of Toby's friends were invited to the party, too. So, Toby asked them to meet at her house so that they all could go to the party together.

Halloween night came at last. When Mrs. Parker called the family to supper, Toby came to the table dressed like a devil. Of course, the little girl's brother and sisters had lots of fun with Toby and Toby enjoyed the fun, too. Before supper was over, the doorbell rang, and into the Parker home came George Washington, two gypsies, a ghost, a cowboy, Little Bo Peep, a fairy queen, a pirate, and a tramp. Then there was real noise and excitement. Everyone was laughing. Everyone talked at the same time. Everyone was happy. Halloween is a night for fun and those children certainly had their share of it.

After some minutes, Mrs. Parker clapped her hands and called for silence. The children wondered what Toby's mother would say.

"Listen, children!" the mother began. "Every night after supper we always say our prayers. So kneel down and join us because Toby must say her prayers before she goes to the party!"

The Parker family knelt down and so did George Washington, the two gypsies, the ghost, the cowboy, Little Bo Peep, the fairy queen, the pirate, and the tramp. Mrs. Parker led the prayers and the others answered her. And all through the prayers Mrs. Parker kept her eye on little Toby dressed like a devil. Mrs. Parker wanted to smile several times but she was very serious. When the prayers were finished, the children with much noise and laughter left for the party and their evening of fun.

When the children were gone, Mrs. Parker sat in

a chair and laughed out loud. The mother laughed so hard that tears came to her eyes.

"What's the matter, Mother?" asked one of the girls. "Why are you laughing?"

The mother waited a moment before she answered. "I'm laughing," she said, "because that's the first time I ever saw the devil on his knees."

Mrs. Parker was right. You never saw the devil on his knees. Neither did I. Any time you have ever seen a picture of the devil, he was always shown as a very proud fellow, standing up against God and daring Him. Yes, the devil is too proud to get down on his knees. If the devil hadn't been so proud in heaven, he wouldn't be in hell today. The devil, you know, was so proud that he thought he was mightier than God. The devil thought he could take God's power away from Him. That's where the devil made his big mistake. He was too proud to obey God and, because of his pride, God punished him. God put the devil out of heaven. God sent the devil to hell.

Pride has made trouble not only for the devil but for many other people. Pride is a terrible sin, a sin that has led many people into other sins. Pride has done plenty of damage to others, and pride will hurt you.

There is one thing that too many children forget. God spreads His gifts around. To one God gives good looks. To another God gives beautiful hair. God gives a beautiful voice to one person. God blesses another person with very fine health. Remember, all these gifts come from God. But some children think they earned these gifts, and because they have these gifts, they think they are better than their neighbors. That's pride. And don't forget that pride is a sin.

If you get good marks on your report card, that's no reason for you to feel that you are smarter than your classmates. You get those good marks because God helps you. If you have prettier dresses than the little girl next door, that doesn't make you better than that little girl. You may have more toys or a larger house than your friends. Well, then, God has been good to you. If you play baseball better than your companions, it's because God helps you. Why, then, should you go around telling people how great you are? Don't be proud and don't be a bragger!

Children, no one likes a child who is proud. If you are proud, God won't like it and your friends won't like you, either. Try to be humble at all times! Then, God will love you and your friends will love you, too. Remember that all your gifts come from God! That thought will help you to be humble.

Boys and girls, the devil is trying to get you into hell. One of the tools he uses is the sin of pride. The devil knows what pride did to him. He knows what pride will do to you. When the devil tempts you to be proud, get down on your knees and pray! A child on his knees is never proud.

God bless you and take good care of yourself!

9. The Smallest Gift

TRUE stories are always the best stories. So this morning I'm going to tell you a true story. Now, I can't tell you the real name of the girl in the story, so we are going to call her Helen Lane.

It was two weeks before Christmas and, like other little girls, nine-year-old Helen was thinking about Christmas. She wondered what she would buy her mother for Christmas. Helen had saved her pennies for some time and altogether she had twenty cents. What could she buy for twenty cents? The little girl wanted to buy something very nice for her mother because she knew that her mother deserved something extra special. Helen thought and thought and she wondered. Then she went to her aunt and asked her aunt to help. Sure enough, the aunt was only too willing to help. In fact, the aunt promised to take Helen shopping the very next day. They would look at all the beautiful things in the stores and then Helen could buy her present.

The next day Helen and her aunt went shopping. Oh, they saw many beautiful presents in the stores, but the presents all cost too much. After all, Helen

had only twenty cents to spend for her present, and you know you can't buy very much for twenty cents. After lunch Helen and her aunt went into the dime store and there Helen found something that she knew would please her mother. A beautiful necklace! A necklace that shone like diamonds! A grand necklace that cost twenty cents! Yes, Helen bought the necklace and she was very happy. Now she knew that her mother would have a grand Christmas. Helen could hardly wait for Christmas to come.

Well, Christmas did come, and there was great excitement in the Lane home on Christmas morning. After Mass Helen and her family had breakfast, and then all of the family gave their presents to one another. There were all kinds of boxes to be opened, all kinds of packages for everyone, but Helen kept her present for her mother until last. When all the packages were opened, Helen gave her mother her little gift.

Mrs. Lane smiled as she started to unwrap the small package. When she opened the box, it was a little while before she could speak. Inside the box was a necklace of glass beads that shone like diamonds. The price tag was still on the necklace and it read — twenty cents.

Helen's mother received some grand gifts that Christmas morning but her best gift was her smallest gift. Her best gift was a necklace of glass beads that shone like diamonds. A necklace that told the mother that her little girl loved her!

Children, the Blessed Virgin is your mother. When Jesus hung on the cross, didn't He give Mary to the world to be everyone's mother? He certainly did! And Mary has been a very good mother to you. Isn't it true that any time you ever wanted anything, you went to Mary and she got it for you? Every time you went to Mary, she was right on the job to help you. Mary always helps her children.

Now, a twenty-cent necklace isn't very much, but it pleased a little girl's mother. Wouldn't you like to give something to Mary, your mother? You can give Mary something better than a necklace of glass beads. You can give her a Hail Mary now and then. You can give her many Hail Marys each day. That's the way to prove that you love Mary.

It doesn't take much time to say a Hail Mary. It takes less than half a minute. And think of all the minutes you have each day! You could give many of those minutes to Mary. Why not start today and see how many Hail Marys you can give to Mary? Then do the same thing tomorrow, and the day after tomorrow, and every single day. Make every day a Hail Mary day, a day filled with Hail Marys. That's the way to show Mary that you love her and are thinking about her. That's the way to show Mary that you want her to think about you.

The Blessed Virgin is a good one to keep on your side, because Mary is very close to Jesus, and Mary has great power in heaven. Mary is your mother and every good mother, you know, takes good care of her children. Mary will take good care of you, if you will pray to her often. Stay close to Mary, and you won't get very far away from God!

God bless you and take good care of yourself!

10. A Pair of Slippers

A LONG time ago I told you a story about the great and mighty Chief Ali Pash who lived far away in Arabia. This morning I want to tell you another story about the same Chief Ali Pash. I hope you will like it!

It seems that one day the great Chief Ali Pash went for a walk in the beautiful garden of his palace. And what do you think happened? Chief Ali Pash stubbed his toe and fell. Now, it's a terrible thing when anyone stubs his toe and falls, and it's even worse when it happens to a great person like Chief Ali Pash. Of course, that fall hurt the great Chief and he flew into a rage. Then and there Chief Ali Pash decided that he would never again stub his toe and fall.

I suppose you are wondering just what Chief Ali Pash did. Well, the Chief called together all of his soldiers and servants and ordered them to lay a carpet over all the paths in his garden and over all the walks of his country.

In that way the great Chief felt that, wherever

[44]

he would walk, he would always walk on a carpet and would never again stub his toe and fall.

When the soldiers and servants heard the order of the great Chief, they shook their heads. They knew that they couldn't lay carpet over the whole country. Some of the soldiers and servants even dared to tell the Chief that they couldn't carry out his order. They couldn't lay carpet over all the walks and paths of the country. They told the Chief that he couldn't always walk on a carpet and that he would just have to be careful. Of course, those soldiers and servants were punished. They were thrown into prison.

Chief Ali Pash waited and waited. He waited several days and nothing was done. Wasn't there someone who could lay carpet over all the walks and paths of the country? Finally, the great Chief offered a reward. Chief Ali Pash promised to give a bag of gold to the person who would help him so that, wherever he walked, he would always walk on a carpet.

Several weeks passed. Then one day a stranger appeared at the gates of the castle of the great Chief Ali Pash. The stranger wanted to see the Chief. The stranger had good news for Chief Ali Pash.

"I have come to get your reward," said the stranger as he stood before the great Chief. "I have come for the bag of gold. I have found how, wherever you walk, you can always walk on a carpet."

Chief Ali Pash looked at the stranger with surprise. "This is good news!" said the great Chief. "If you show me how I can always walk on carpet, you shall have the bag of gold. If you fail, you shall spend the rest of your days in prison."

The stranger smiled. The stranger knew that he couldn't fail. He knew that he would win the bag of gold. And do you know what the stranger did? The stranger opened his cloak and took out a pair of slippers. Now those slippers were not ordinary slippers. Oh, no! Those slippers were made of carpet and they were lined with soft wool. Then the stranger knelt down and put the carpet slippers on the feet of the great Chief Ali Pash.

Chief Ali Pash walked a few steps, smiled, and nodded his head. "You have won my reward!" he said to the stranger. "You have won the bag of gold!"

And forever after, the great Chief Ali Pash was happy. No matter where he walked, he always wore his slippers made of carpet. And so the Chief always walked on carpet. It was all very simple. Wasn't it?

Would you like to walk through life with a happy heart? Would you like to walk through life without worries, without being afraid? I'm sure you would, children, and it's very easy. Now I'm not going to tell you to walk through life wearing a pair of carpet slippers. No, there's something better than carpet slippers. If you want to walk through life without worries and with a happy heart, keep your soul in the state of grace!

Who are the people who are not happy? Who are

the people who are afraid? People who have mortal sins on their souls! You can't be happy without God and, if there is mortal sin on your soul, God is not there. People who have mortal sins on their souls are afraid because they have lost God. They know that, if they die with mortal sins, they will lose their souls and they will lose God forever. No wonder they are afraid!

Children, if you should ever make the mistake of falling into mortal sin, go to confession as soon as you can! Get that mortal sin off your soul and bring God back into your soul! Don't take any chances! God wants to live in your soul at all times, and He will live there if your soul is in the state of grace.

Boys and girls, do you want to be happy in this world? Do you want to be happy with God in heaven? Then, keep your soul in the state of grace! The state of grace will take you to God with a happy heart.

God bless you and take good care of yourself!

11. Six Red Roses

LAST Tuesday afternoon I went for a ride in my car. It was a beautiful afternoon and I thought I would enjoy a ride in the country. Well, I did enjoy the ride. I enjoyed it very much. Little did I think, however, when I left the house last Tuesday, that I would come back with a story. Here's what happened!

I was driving through a small town on my way home when I saw a flower shop. I knew that we needed flowers for the altar, so I decided to stop. I went into the flower shop, walked around, and admired the flowers. Before I bought any flowers, the door opened and a little boy came into the shop.

The boy was about ten years old and he was dressed in overalls. His red hair was mussed and his shirt was dirty. The boy carried a paper bag in his hand.

"Well, young man," said the flower lady very politely, "is there something that I can do for you?"

"Yes!" answered the little boy and he held up his paper bag. "I just emptied my piggy bank. How many flowers can I buy for ninety-four cents?"

The flower lady's eyes opened wide and she tried not to smile. "Flowers cost lots of money," she said, "but what kind would you like?"

The little fellow walked around the store and looked at the many flowers. The boy liked all the flowers, but he liked, especially, the beautiful red roses.

"Lady," he asked, "how much are the red roses?"

"The red roses," she answered, "are two dollars a dozen. Now if you want six of them, you can have them for ninety-four cents."

The boy was pleased. "Thanks, lady!" he said. "I'll take six of your very best red roses."

The flower lady picked out six large red roses, put them in a box, and covered the roses with soft paper. "Now what do you want me to write on the card?" she asked.

The little boy thought for a moment. "Please write on the card," he said, " 'Happy Birthday, Mother!' "

The flower lady wrote on the card just what the boy wanted. Then she placed the card on top of the soft paper, covered the box, and tied the box with string. She didn't bother counting the ninety-four pennies when the little boy handed her his precious bag. The flower lady and I smiled at each other as the little fellow walked proudly out of the shop with his box of six red roses.

Now that's not the end of the story! I spent some time in the flower shop and then went next door to buy some cigars. Then I went to another store and bought some fruit. When I finished my shopping, I started for home.

As I was driving slowly through the end of the town, whom do you think I saw? I saw the same little boy with the red hair and overalls walking along and still carrying under his arm his box of six red roses. The little boy was going through the gates of a small country cemetery.

Do you know that several times this week I have thought about that boy and his six red roses. I wish I knew that boy's name, and I hope that some day I shall meet him again, because I'd like to shake his hand. There is a lot of good in that little fellow. That boy didn't forget his best friend even though she was dead. He still wanted to be good to his mother. It must have been hard for him to empty his piggy bank, but he wanted to make his mother happy. That's why my little friend bought six red roses.

Each one of you must know someone who has died. Maybe your grandfather, your grandmother, your aunt, your uncle, or your father or mother is no longer alive. When that person was alive, he may have been very good to you. Now that person is gone. Have you forgotten that person already? Wouldn't you like to make that person happy? Well, you can help that person and you can make that person very happy. How? Well, you won't have to empty your piggy bank. All that you have to do is to pray for that person's soul.

You can help the souls in purgatory with your prayers and you can even get your friends out of purgatory with your prayers. Red roses are very beautiful, but don't forget that red roses can't help the dead. Red roses will never get a soul out of purgatory. Prayer, however, will help the dead and the souls in purgatory.

It may be that you don't know any person who has died. If that is true, then you shouldn't stop praying for the souls in purgatory. Don't forget that there are thousands of souls in purgatory who have no one to pray for them. You can pray for those souls and you can get them out of purgatory. The souls in purgatory, you know, can't pray for themselves. They have to suffer for a certain length of time and, when you pray for them, you shorten their time in purgatory. Can't you see, then, that prayers for the dead help more than red roses?

I think that the little boy in the overalls has taught us a very important lesson. He has taught us to remember the dead. I'm sure that the little fellow who bought six red roses for his mother didn't forget to pray for her, too. If that boy's mother was not already in heaven with God, then the boy helped her with his prayers. One of the best ways to remember the dead, one of the best ways to help the dead is with your prayers.

God bless you and take good care of yourself!

12. A Surprise for a King

A KING, you know, receives many gifts, and very often these presents are worth hundreds of dollars. It may be a gift of money, diamonds, jewels, or precious stones. Then, too, a king may receive a very small gift. Well, one day King Louis received a small gift, a gift that didn't cost very much money, but that small gift meant more to the King than diamonds, silver, or gold.

King Louis was a very friendly King, a King who loved his people. Best of all, King Louis loved little children, and King Louis thought that the little children in his country were the best little children in the world. That's why the King built so many beautiful schools for his children. He built parks and playgrounds for his little friends. He had parties for the children, and every summer the King had a picnic to which he invited all the children of his country.

The King's picnic was always a big day for little boys and girls. That was the day when boys and girls had plenty of free ice cream, cake, and pink lemonade. It was a day for races and games. The day when the children saw a real circus! That was the day when the children saw King Louis and even talked to him. The day when the children shook the King's hand!

Now little Mary Huebner was just as excited as her other little friends. Mary thought that the day for the King's picnic would never come. But picnic day did come, and Mary had a wonderful time at the King's picnic. She ran races, played games, and even won a prize. The little girl laughed at the funny clowns in the circus and clapped hard when the bears danced. Of course, Mary ate plenty of ice cream and cake and drank three glasses of pink lemonade. Mary Huebner enjoyed every minute at the picnic and the little girl certainly had lots of fun.

When the picnic was over, all the children stood in line and each child shook the King's hand. Of course, most of the children thanked the King for being so kind.

Little Mary stood in line, too, and she could hardly wait for her turn to shake the King's hand. After all, King Louis was a mighty important person to little Mary. No wonder Mary's little heart pounded inside her! No wonder Mary was nervous!

At last, it was Mary's turn to shake the King's hand. The little girl looked up at the King and smiled, and the King smiled back at the little girl.

"Did you have a nice time at the picnic?" asked the King as he shook Mary's hand.

"Oh, I had a grand time," answered the little girl, "and thank you very much!"

Then little Mary did something that certainly surprised the King. The little girl offered the King the only thing she had in this world. "Please take this!" she begged. "I want you to have it."

The King's eyes almost popped out of his head. He smiled, nodded his head, and took the present from the little girl. In a moment, little Mary Huebner was gone, and King Louis stood admiring the present he had received from the child, an old, worn-out doll.

King Louis received many presents during his life, but he kept only one of them on the desk where he did most of his work. Many times each day the King looked at that present and smiled. And many times each day the King thought about Mary Huebner, the little girl who loved her King so much that she gave him the only thing she had in this world, an old, worn-out doll.

Children, Christ is your King, and Christ has done so much to show that He loves you. Christ came on this earth because He loves you. Christ suffered and died on the cross because He loves you. Christ lives in our church because He loves you. Christ even lets you receive Him in Holy Communion. Why? Because He loves you and wants to be near you! Yes, Christ, your King, loves little children, all children. Christ, your King, loves you.

Now what about you? Do you love Christ, your King? Oh, I know that you tell Christ you love Him, but do you show your love? I don't mean that you have to give Christ an old, worn-out doll. Christ doesn't need and doesn't want your old, worn-out doll. But there is one present that you can give Christ, a present that will show Him that you really love Him. That present is a clean soul, a soul free from sin.

How can you keep your soul free from sin? By obeying Christ's laws! By keeping the Commandments! There are only ten of them, you know, ten Commandments or ten laws. Keep those ten laws and you will have a clean soul! That's the way to show Christ that you love Him. That's the best present you can give Christ, your King.

Little Mary Huebner showed King Louis that she loved him by giving him an old, worn-out doll. Are you going to show Christ, your King, that you love Him by keeping your soul free from sin? I hope so!

God bless you and take good care of yourself!

13. The Three Little Angels

DO YOU know that Halloween can be just like Thanksgiving and Christmas? Well, I found out this year. Yes, Halloween can be just like Thanksgiving and Christmas. Listen!

This year on Halloween night I was ready. I was ready and waiting for the ghosts, goblins, and witches who I knew would ring my doorbell. Well, they didn't disappoint me. Just as soon as I finished my supper, the doorbell began to ring, and it rang most of the evening. Every time I went to the door, I found ghosts, witches, and goblins, who said they would play tricks on me if I didn't treat. Of course, I didn't want my ghost friends playing tricks, so I treated. It was an evening of fun for the children and I enjoyed it, too. Even though I was afraid sometimes, I couldn't help but laugh at the funny clothes the children wore. Halloween night was certainly a busy one for me, but I had lots of fun.

About nine o'clock the doorbell stopped ringing. I waited and waited but there were no more rings. "I guess 'tricks or treats' is over for another year," I said to myself as I picked up the evening paper and began to read. Then, all of a sudden, the door-bell rang. "More 'tricks or treats,'" I thought as I hurried to the door. And was I surprised? When I opened the door, I found three beautiful little angels standing on the porch carrying baskets. I almost forgot and almost called the angels by name because those three little angels were pupils from the fourth grade of Saint Bridget's School.

"Father," said the angel in the middle, and she must have known that I was surprised, "we're not playing 'tricks or treats.' We're getting treats for others and we want to make some children happy. Will you give us something for the poor?"

For a moment I could hardly believe my ears. There, standing before me, were three little angels of mercy, three little angels begging for treats, not for themselves but for others. That was something new to me, something that touched my heart. I was proud of my three little angels because their hearts were right. Those little angels gave up their own treats on Halloween night so that they could treat others. Now doesn't that prove that Halloween can be just like Thanksgiving and Christmas?

I knew it was late, but I made my three little angels come into the house. First of all, I wanted them to have a treat. I called my housekeeper and she prepared a lunch, and my fourth-grade angels drank hot chocolate and ate coconut cake. Do you know that that was the first time I ever had a chance to treat three angels? If the angels in heaven are anything like

my fourth-grade ones, I'm going to try harder than ever to get to heaven. It's going to be worth it.

After they finished the lunch, my little angels thought that I forgot something. Well, I didn't forget. I didn't forget their three baskets. No, sir! I hurried around the house and gathered everything I thought poor children could use. Canned fruit, canned soup, oranges, bananas, soap, toothpaste, pencils, candy, nuts, rosaries, medals, and holy pictures, all these went into the three baskets. Oh, I wish you could have seen the faces of the angels while I filled their baskets! I'm sure they were happy, but not half as happy as I was.

"Thanks, Father, for everything!" said my three little friends as I led them to the door. And three little angels with three happy hearts and three filled baskets walked out into the dark night to make the world brighter for others.

Children, life has been unkind to thousands of little children in this world. There are thousands of boys and girls in this world who are poor and who are suffering. We like to pretend the ghosts, goblins, and witches come out only on Halloween night. But there are places in this world where the ghosts of fear, the witches of cold, and the goblins of hunger come out every night. Some poor children have sad tricks played on them every day and every night. Some food, some warm clothing, some soap to wash away the dirt, an old doll or a toy, these are the treats that chase away the tricks of suffering.

Do you know any little boy or girl who is poor? Do you know someone who may be suffering? Oh, you must know someone because there are so many of them. Well, then, why don't you help? You can at least be kind to the poor. You can play with them and help them to forget their troubles. Yes, and I am sure that most of you can do something more. I think that, if you would speak to your parents, they would help you to be kind to the poor. Maybe you have some good warm clothes that are too small for you now. Some poor child would be very happy to get those clothes. Maybe one little orange or an old baseball would make some child happy. You don't have to wait until Christmas to do kind deeds. You can do them every day. It's just a matter of thinking about others, helping others, trying to make it easy for others.

Why don't you pick out some boy or girl whom you can help? Just try and see how much good you can do for that child! You will not only make that child happy by your kindness, but you will also make yourself very happy. Try it and see whether I am right!

I would like to make this new way of playing "tricks or treats" a game for every boy and girl to play. I would like to see all of you play this game not only on Halloween but every day. It's the game of thinking of others, the game of helping others. You may not have wings and you may not be a real angel, but you can be an angel of mercy, a guardian angel for others.

Now if your doorbell rings some night and you find one of my fourth-grade angels standing on your porch, you will know what to do.

God bless you and take good care of yourself!

14. The First Watch

THIS morning I want to tell you a story that happened over four hundred and fifty years ago. I want to tell you about Peter Henlein who lived in Germany. Peter was a locksmith, a man who made and repaired locks for doors. He was a hard worker, a faithful worker, and every day Peter was busy in his little shop.

One day while working in his shop, Peter had an idea. Of course, we all have ideas and we soon forget them. But not Peter Henlein! Peter thought about his idea for months and months. Then he wrote his idea on paper and even drew pictures. He made plans and, from time to time, he changed them. Night after night through many long months Peter thought and planned, and during all that time he kept his idea to himself.

It's a good thing that Peter was patient. After he planned well and figured out everything in his mind, Peter began to work. He worked with little wheels, little springs, and tiny screws. First, he arranged the wheels and springs one way and they would not work. Then, he tried another way, and still they wouldn't work. This went on time and time again. Another man would have given up and would have forgotten the whole thing, but Peter refused to quit. The locksmith wouldn't give up because he knew that he had a good idea, and he was certain that his idea would work.

Well, one night after months of hard work and disappointment, Peter worked later than usual. He worked with his little wheels, springs, and tiny screws, all held together in a little case. All of a sudden, he turned a small wheel on the top of the case and then held the case to his ear. At first, Peter could hardly believe what he heard. He jumped to his feet and his heart almost stopped beating. Then he held the case to his ear again. Yes, it was true! Peter heard tick, tock, tick, tock, come steadily from the little case.

"Thank God!" he cried out loud. "My work is done. I've made the first watch!"

Even though he was tired and weary, Peter Henlein didn't sleep a wink that night. He was too excited to sleep. Too happy to sleep! He could hardly wait for morning to come. But morning did come and Peter was up bright and early. Long before anyone appeared on the street, Peter took everything out of the window of his little shop. Then he placed his watch in the center of the window where people could see.

Well, there was great excitement in Peter's town

that morning. Hundreds of people stopped to look at the first watch. And for months and months, no one ever passed Peter's shop without looking at the watch. Some people thought that some day the watch would stop running. But Peter took good care of his watch. He wound it every day, kept it clean, and handled it very carefully. That's why the watch ran so well. It never ran too fast and it was never slow. No wonder Peter Henlein was proud and happy!

Well, one day a very rich man went into Peter's shop. "I've come," said the man, "to buy your watch."

At first, Peter was surprised. Peter didn't want to sell his treasure. But when the rich man offered a large sum of money, the locksmith decided to sell the watch. Peter took the man's money and then carefully wrapped the watch in soft cloth. As he handed the precious package to the man, there was a tear in Peter's eye.

"Take good care of this watch," said Peter, "and it will always be right! Wind it every day, keep it clean, and never shake it too hard! Keep it away from the heat and don't let it get too cold! If you follow these simple rules, you'll have no trouble with the watch."

The rich man thanked Peter for his good advice and promised to follow his directions. The new owner followed the rules carefully and the watch kept perfect time. But one day the rich man forgot to wind the watch. So do you know what happened? The watch stopped.

Now answer this question! Who was to blame because the watch stopped? Was Peter to blame or was it the fault of the rich man? Of course, it was the rich man's fault. The watch stopped because the rich man didn't wind it. The watch stopped because the rich man didn't follow the rules.

Children, long ago Almighty God had an idea, and God thought about His idea for a long time. God planned and planned and then God did something. God made this world. Then God made people to live on this earth, and God made you. When God made you, He put a soul in your body and your soul will live forever. Now God wants you to take good care of your soul so that after your death your soul will surely go to heaven. So do you know what God has done? God has given you ten rules to follow and we call God's rules the Ten Commandments. If you follow God's Commandments, if you keep God's rules, you will surely save your soul.

God didn't give you Ten Commandments just to make it hard for you. Oh, no! God gave you Ten Commandments to help you, to keep you out of trouble. The watchmaker gave the rich man a few rules to follow so that the watch would always be right. God did the same thing. God gave you rules to follow to protect you.

Remember, your soul is the most important part of you. Your soul is much more important than your body. Therefore, you should take good care of your soul. You should take more care of your soul than you do of your body. And the best way to take care of your soul is to follow God's rules.

So, then, look on the Ten Commandments as helps. The Commandments will help you to get to heaven. If the rich man had followed the rules, his watch would not have stopped. If you follow God's rules, you will save your soul and your soul will live forever with God.

God bless you and take good care of yourself!

15. The Moon's Secret

LONG, long ago, in the land of silver clouds, there lived a beautiful little star by the name of Flasher. Night after night Flasher shone in the sky and smiled down from the heavens on little boys and girls. Flasher was a hard-working star and very serious.

Now, there was one thing that bothered Flasher very much. He worried about the Man in the Moon. Flasher knew that the Moon had been shining in the sky for thousands of years. He knew that the Man in the Moon was old and tired and deserved a rest. So little Flasher decided to offer his help.

One night little Flasher skipped across the sky. It was a long trip over to the Moon, but Flasher was excited. He stopped several times to catch his breath, but finally he reached the Moon. Flasher wondered whether the Moon would be angry because the little star left his place in the sky. But the Moon was not angry. In fact, the Moon smiled at the little star and was pleased to see him.

"Oh, Mister Moon," said the little star, "you must be tired. Why don't you take it easy? Let me take your place for a little while and you can take a rest!"

Of course, the Moon was surprised and he smiled to himself. Then the Moon became very sad. "I'm not as young as I used to be," he said, "and I'm very tired. Night after night I light up the world and it's a big job. Little children look for me and I can't disappoint them."

"Oh, but it's late now and little children are in bed," answered the little star. "If you'll take a rest," he promised, "I'll shine brighter than ever."

The Man in the Moon thought for a moment and then nodded his head. "All right!" he said. "We'll try it for a while and we'll see what happens."

So the Man in the Moon climbed behind a cloud and soon he was fast asleep. And the little star flashed and shone brighter than ever before. And I don't have to tell you that Flasher was happy because he was so important, happy because he was lighting up the world, happy because he was taking the Moon's place.

Of course, men and women looked up at the sky that night but they saw no Moon. People wondered what had happened to the Man in the Moon. Was the old man sick? If people had known the Moon's secret, they would have smiled. But little Flasher kept the secret and worked hard while the tired old Moon took a rest.

When the Moon awoke, he felt better, but he was a shy old Moon when he peeked from behind the cloud and went to work again. He thanked the little star for being so kind and Flasher skipped back to his right place in the sky.

Now, that was only the beginning. Down through the years little Flasher has changed places with the Moon many, many times. Many a night when little boys and girls have been asleep, the Moon has been sleeping, too. The Moon has slept behind the clouds and Flasher has done his work. And best of all, Flasher has never told anyone, and I don't want you to tell anyone either, because that's the Moon's secret.

So some night when all is quiet and still, look up at the sky! You may not see the Moon, because the Moon will be behind a cloud — sleeping. But if you try real hard, you may see little Flasher up there helping the Moon.

Then, too, when you look up at the sky, you may see the Moon shining brightly. If you look long enough, the Man in the Moon may smile at you and he may even wink. If the Man in the Moon ever smiles at you, that will be a sign that he knows that you know his secret. If the Man in the Moon ever winks at you, that will be a sign, too, that you have kept the Moon's secret.

Children, Flasher is only a little star in the sky, but he has a very big heart. That's why I like him. Flasher does his own job and he helps the Moon, too. He makes it easy for the Moon. I'll bet that Flasher is one of the happiest stars in the sky and I think that Flasher can teach you a lesson.

You are small, too, but you can help others and you can be kind to others. You can help right in your own home. You can help your mother with the dusting. You can help set the table. Many of you can help with the dishes. You can cut the grass, pick up papers in the yard, and run errands. Why, there are many ways you can help around the house. Don't expect your father and mother to do everything!

Do you ever think about the lady next door? Isn't there some way you can help her and make it easier for her? What about school? Do you help the janitor by keeping papers off the floor? Do you ever offer to help Sister after school? Maybe you can help some boy or girl in your class who finds it hard to learn. If you'll look around, you'll find many people who need help.

Now, don't expect to get paid in money or something like that for every kind act you do! Kindness doesn't mean working for pay. Don't forget that God will see every kind act and God will pay you well. Learn to think about others! Be kind to the poor and be kind to old people! Help others every chance you get! Remember that God said that if we do something good to others, we really do it to Him!

Flasher is the Moon's best helper. If you help others, you will be a little Flasher.

God bless you and take good care of yourself!

16. A Home for Kip

GEORGE and Judy Slate had a dog. And the dog was their best friend. The children loved their dog and they took very good care of him. They fed the dog, gave him baths, and put him to bed at night. You can see that George, Judy, and the dog were very good pals.

Well, one day the children's mother told them that they would have to get rid of the dog. That was bad news. It was sad news. And the children were heartbroken. They begged their mother to let them keep the dog, but the mother wouldn't listen. The mother wouldn't change her mind. So the next morning little George and Judy left the house with their dog. Some time later George and Judy came home alone.

I suppose you are wondering what happened to the dog. Well, the children tied the dog to the handle of the door at the city pound for animals, and they fastened a note to his collar. Here's what the note said:

"Dear Mr. Dog Catcher:

"We are two little children and our mother won't let us keep our dog because it costs too much to feed him.

"The dog's name is Kip and he is one year old. He walks by your side and obeys. He's friendly and doesn't bite.

"We love Kip and want to keep him, but we have to be brave. We brought Kip here ourselves. The dog cried and so did we. Please find a good home for Kip and we'll pray for you every night!

"George and Judy."

When the Dog Catcher read the children's note, he didn't try to find a home for the dog. He knew that Kip belonged in one place and no other place. He knew that Kip should be with George and Judy. So do you know what the Dog Catcher did? You'll never guess! The Dog Catcher put Kip's picture in the paper. And that isn't all! Right under the dog's picture the man put the children's letter.

Then what happened? Well, thousands of people saw the dog's picture and thousands of people read the children's letter. Some people smiled and soon forgot about the children and their dog. But a good many people wanted to do something. A good many people wanted to help George, Judy, and Kip, and they did help. What did the good people do? Why, they sent boxes and boxes of dog biscuits to George and Judy, and some people even sent money. They sent money so that the children could buy carrots, milk, and meat for their dog. The strangers wanted

George and Judy to have their dog. They wanted Kip to be with his friends.

Now here's the best part of the story! When the children's mother saw the kindness of strangers, she changed her mind. And today George and Judy Slate are the two happiest children in this great city. George and Judy are happy because, once again, they have Kip.

That's the way every story should end! I think that George and Judy were paid back because they did what they were told. When their mother gave an order, the children obeyed. It was hard for those children to give up their best friend, but they obeyed their mother, and because they obeyed, the children were paid back.

Many boys and girls find it hard to obey. When their parents or teachers give an order, they don't like it. Now your parents and teachers never give an order just to make it hard for you. They never give an order just to make you unhappy. Your parents and teachers usually have a very good reason for giving an order, and very often they are trying to keep you from harm. Of course, you don't understand that and you pout and disobey. That's where you make a mistake and that's where you sin. If you would only realize that your parents and teachers are working for your good, then you wouldn't disobey. Don't forget that your parents and teachers know a great deal more than you do. They know what is good for you even though you don't understand. So when your parents or teachers ask you to do something, obey!

What do you do when your parents and teachers ask you to help them? Do you obey? Well, I hope you do. After all, your parents and teachers work very hard for you. They are always trying to help you. They are always doing something for you. Shouldn't you, then, try to help them? Just think how hard your father works every day! Think of the many things your mother does every day! Think how hard your teacher works to help you! Do your parents or teachers ask you to work just as hard for them? I should say not! Your parents and teachers only ask you to help them. They only ask you to do little things.

You may never be asked to give up your dog, but when your parents or teachers ask you to do something, obey, and obey right away! That's the way to please God. Then in pleasing God you will be sure to please your parents and teachers.

God bless you and take good care of yourself!

17. A Bag of Gold Marbles

WHEN I was a boy, I didn't spend my nights listening to the radio or watching television. There was no such thing as radio in those days and there was no television. But just the same, we had fun at our house. We played games and read books, and Sunday night was always story night. That was the night when my father always told one of his famous stories. Maybe you would like to hear one of those stories, the story about Terry and the bag of gold marbles.

Terry O'Donnell was a little Irish boy and, like all boys who lived in Ireland, he believed in giants and fairies and little men who lived under the ground. But Terry O'Donnell had never seen a giant. He had never seen a fairy. He had never seen one of the little men of Ireland. No, not until that summer day when Terry went fishing! That day Terry had the surprise of his life.

Terry fished all morning and caught nothing. He was tired and disgusted and started for home. The boy had gone only a little way when he heard someone call his name. Terry stopped, looked around, but could see no one.

"Where are you?" called Terry at the top of his voice.

There was no answer at first, but then a tiny little man jumped out from behind a bush. When Terry saw the little fellow, his eyes almost popped out of his head. The tiny little man was only about two feet tall. He was real, though, and very much alive.

"Do you live under the ground?" Terry asked excitedly.

The tiny little man smiled and nodded his head. "Yes," he answered, "I live under the ground. Would you like to see my home?"

Terry didn't have to be asked a second time. Certainly he wanted to see the little man's home! Terry thought that would be lots of fun.

Terry followed the tiny little man through the woods. Now maybe you think that Terry was afraid. Well, Terry wasn't afraid because he was curious. Suddenly, the tiny man stopped walking. He stooped down and picked up a small red stone, and hidden under the stone was a shining button. The little man pushed the button and guess what happened! A large piece of earth opened up just like a door!

By this time Terry wondered whether it was all a dream. But it wasn't a dream! Terry was wide awake! Terry followed the little man down a long stairway. When they reached the bottom of the stairs, the little man pushed another button and the door at the top of the stairs closed.

Was it dark down under the earth? Not at all! It was almost as bright as day because the one large room was lighted by lanterns, candles, and colored lights. There were tiny tables and tiny chairs, tiny beds and a tiny stove. Everything in the room was small and all the people were small. Why, there must have been twenty tiny people living in that great big room and they were all very happy. The tiny people were pleased because Terry had come to visit them.

Of course, the tiny little people prepared a meal for Terry and what a grand meal it was! Terry was hungry and he enjoyed the good food. Oh, how he laughed at the funny stories told by the strange little men! He liked their songs, too. Yes, Terry O'Donnell had a grand time. It was all so different.

After dinner the tiny little men washed the dishes and they wouldn't let Terry help. So Terry walked around the large room and looked at the many strange things. A tiny piano! A small bicycle! And there was one thing, especially, that caught Terry's eye. It was a small bag of gold marbles.

When Terry saw those marbles, he wanted them. Yes, Terry wanted those marbles for himself. So what do you think? Terry took the bag of gold marbles from the shelf and put the bag in his pocket.

When the tiny little men finished their work, they played the piano and sang songs. They played a few games and told more stories. They were certainly nice people who tried hard to please their new friend. But Terry was worried. Terry was ashamed.

The tiny little men had been good to Terry, but he had stolen their bag of gold marbles.

Finally, Terry decided to go home. He thanked the tiny little men and they followed him to the door. Terry waved his hand and started through the woods. When the boy was out of sight, he took the bag of marbles from his pocket and opened it. Boy, they were beautiful marbles! The finest marbles Terry had ever seen! He closed the bag and, holding the bag in his hand, started to run. But just as Terry ran into his yard, he stumbled, fell, and dropped the bag of precious marbles. And what do you think? Before Terry could pick himself up, one of the tiny little men grabbed the bag of marbles and hurried away. Yes, he had seen Terry steal the marbles and had followed him.

Terry O'Donnell was just like so many boys and girls. His eyes were too big. Those marbles didn't belong to Terry and he had no right to touch them. He took something that didn't belong to him. When Terry stole those marbles, he thought that no one saw him. But one of the tiny little men saw everything, and I'm mighty happy that the little man got back his bag of gold marbles.

Boys and girls, you have no right to touch anything that doesn't belong to you. When you take something that doesn't belong to you, you steal, and stealing is a sin. When you steal, you may think that no one sees you, but don't forget that God sees you. And another thing! Whenever you steal, it is not enough to tell the sin of stealing in confession. You must do something more. You must always give back the thing that was stolen. If you don't give back the stolen thing, or make up for it in some way, your sin will not be forgiven.

Children, be satisfied with what God has given you! If you want something, ask your parents for it, and if Mother and Dad say "no," then go without it. If little Terry had asked for the gold marbles, maybe the little men would have given them to him. Don't be like Terry O'Donnell! *Don't steal!*

God bless you and take good care of yourself!

[78]

18. A Surprise from Santa Claus

SEVEN-YEAR-OLD Bobby Shaw lived in Chicago with his mother and two sisters. Bobby liked Chicago because he had lived there all his life. But there was one thing that Bobby didn't like. Bobby didn't like to have his father working so far away from home. Bobby's father worked and lived away up in Alaska and that meant that the little fellow didn't see his dad very often. In fact, Bobby hadn't seen his father for a year and a half, and that's a long time for a boy to be away from his dad.

Well, it was early in December and, like all boys, Bobby was thinking about Christmas. Oh, Bobby wanted many things for Christmas, but there was one thing that the little boy wanted more than anything else in this world. Bobby wanted to be with his dad for Christmas. Bobby thought about the fun he could have and the more he thought about it, the more the boy wanted his father for Christmas.

Now, Bobby knew that Santa Claus would fly down from the North Pole on Christmas Eve and visit the homes of good boys and girls. That gave the little fellow an idea. So what did Bobby do but write a letter to Santa Claus! He asked Santa to give him a ride in his plane on his way back to the North Pole, and Bobby asked Santa to drop him off in Alaska.

Of course, Santa Claus received Bobby's letter and the jolly old fellow smiled when he read it. Santa knew that Bobby wanted to go to his father so that he could be with him for Christmas. But Santa had a better idea. Santa planned a surprise and he kept it a secret.

I suppose Santa Claus was too busy to answer Bobby's letter and the little fellow was certainly disappointed. The boy thought that maybe his letter had been lost. So Bobby gave up all hope of being with his father for Christmas.

Christmas morning came and little Bobby Shaw awoke bright and early. He jumped out of bed and rushed downstairs to see what Santa had left for him. And was Bobby surprised? There, sitting in a chair next to the Christmas tree, was Bobby's father! Bobby's father had come for Christmas!

How did Bobby's father get all the way home from Alaska? Santa Claus took care of everything. When Santa left the North Pole, he stopped off in Alaska, and Santa brought the father from Alaska to Chicago in his own big plane. So after all his worry, Bobby had his father for Christmas. Bobby Shaw couldn't go to his father, so Bobby's father came to the little boy.

I know that you boys and girls would like to be near God, your Father. You would like to see God.

You would like to talk with Him. But you can't go to God now. You can't see God until He calls you to heaven. Now God knows that you want to be near Him, so do you know what God has done? God has come to you. Yes, that's right! God is living down here on earth. God is living in the tabernacle on every altar in every Catholic church.

It's a grand thing to know and remember that God is so close to us, that God is here in our church. God, our Father, is with us not only on Christmas, but every day. God is here whenever we want Him and the doors of our church are never closed. God wants the doors open so that you can come to Him. God has done His part — He has come down from heaven to our altar. Now you must do the rest!

What does God expect you to do? First of all, God wants you to come to church often. God wants you to visit Him. He wants you to talk to Him. God wants to know all about you and your family. He wants to know how you are getting along in school. He wants to know about your friends who are sick. Your games, your work, your lessons, your home! God wants to know about all these things. Remember, God is your best Friend and He wants to know all about you. So when you visit God in church, be friendly with Him! Your visits don't have to be long. They can be very short, but your visits should be often.

Now there is something else God wants you to do. He wants you to receive Him often in Holy Communion. Just think of it! You can have God leave His home on the altar and come and live right inside your soul. You can have God come to your soul any time you wish. You can have God come every day. Every time you receive Holy Communion, God comes to you. That's why you should receive Holy Communion often.

God doesn't let the angels in heaven receive Holy Communion, but He lets you. Doesn't that prove that God loves you a great deal? It certainly does!

Too many boys and girls think that God lives just up in the sky. But that isn't true! God, our Father, is very close to us because He lives on our altar. Visit Him as much as you can, and let Him come to visit you often in Holy Communion!

God bless you and take good care of yourself!

19. Doorbells

A DOORBELL is a very important part of every home. I know that my doorbell means a great deal to me. When my doorbell rings, immediately I wonder who is standing on the other side of the door. I hurry to the door and open it. Maybe someone wants to ask me some questions. I may learn that someone is sick. I may find a little boy or girl who wants to have a rosary blessed. Every time my doorbell rings, I see a new face, a new person. So my doorbell is an exciting part of my life.

It's the same with you. When your doorbell rings, you drop everything and hurry to the door. You may find the mailman at the door or a man with a package. You may find a man who wants to sell something to your mother. You may find the boy or girl who lives next door. Very, very often the doorbell may bring a surprise. When you open the door, you may find your favorite aunt, or your cousins, and maybe your uncle, too. Yes, when the doorbell rings, there is always excitement.

Now, let's suppose that someday you are at home alone watching TV. The doorbell rings. You wonder who it is and hurry to the door. You open the door and what a surprise! There, standing at your door, is Jesus Christ. What would you do if Jesus rang your doorbell? Oh, I know what you would do. After you caught your breath, you would certainly invite Jesus into your home. You would offer Jesus the most comfortable chair in your living room. You would turn off the TV and forget all about it. Then you would tell Jesus how happy you are to have Him as your Guest.

If Jesus ever came to your house, would you be lost for words? Well, I don't think so! Why, there would be so many things that you would want to tell Jesus. You would tell Jesus about your mother and father. You would talk about your brothers and sisters. You would tell Jesus about school and your teacher and your friends. You'd tell Him about your baseball team and your games. You'd show Jesus your dog and you'd make your dog do some tricks. And I'm pretty sure that you would ask Jesus a good many questions.

You'd ask about heaven. You'd ask Jesus about the Blessed Mother and Saint Joseph. And you would certainly thank Jesus for being so good to you. I know, too, that you would listen to every word that Jesus would speak to you. You would remember everything Jesus would say, and you would enjoy every minute of your visit. If Jesus should ever ring your doorbell, you would be the happiest boy or girl in this world.

Do you know that Jesus wants you to be the happiest boy or girl in this world? Do you know that Jesus rings your doorbell every day? Yes, Jesus wants to come into your house. Jesus wants to come into your soul very often. Jesus rings the doorbell but you are too busy to answer, and because you don't answer, Jesus doesn't visit you very often.

Now don't look at me as though you don't understand! Jesus wants to come into your soul often in Holy Communion, but you lock Jesus out. I know people who open the door for Jesus every morning and receive Him in Holy Communion. Why don't you receive Jesus often? Jesus wants to be with you, but you keep Jesus away. When Jesus rings, you don't answer the door.

I suppose you are thinking that it is hard to get up early on weekdays and go to Mass and receive Holy Communion. Yes, children, it is hard to get up early, but many people do it every day. Keep in mind that you are going to receive Jesus and you won't find it too hard to get up early! Think of all the extra graces you will receive! If you receive Holy Communion often, Jesus will make you a better boy or a better girl. He will help you with your work in school. Jesus will bless your home. He will help you fight against temptations. If you receive Holy Communion often, Jesus will be on your side in everything you do. You can't lose with Jesus. You are bound to come out on top.

I think most boys and girls want to do the right

thing. Most boys and girls want to go to heaven. Most boys and girls want to avoid sin. But what happens? Every so often boys and girls fall into sin. Why do they fall into sin? They fall into sin because Jesus isn't near to help them. They close the door in His face and then wonder why He isn't there to help them. If those boys and girls received Jesus often in Holy Communion, Jesus would be right with them to help them fight against temptations. Yes, children, Holy Communion helps you to keep away from sin. Holy Communion makes it much easier for you to get to heaven.

The more you know Jesus, the more you will love Him. The more you love Jesus, the harder you will try to keep away from sin. Now, if you will receive Jesus often, you will certainly get to know Him better. You will have more visits with Jesus, and Jesus will have more visits with you. In a word, by receiving Holy Communion often, Jesus and you will become very close friends. Would you want anything better? I don't think so!

Children, this week Jesus wants you to receive Him in Holy Communion. Maybe Jesus will ring your doorbell tomorrow morning. Are you going to let Jesus in?

God bless you and take good care of yourself!

20. The Two Magic Gifts

LONG, long ago there lived a great King by the name of Alexander. King Alexander had two very close friends, one a soldier and the other a doctor. Now, the King liked both friends very much, but the King often wondered which friend was the more faithful. So one day the King decided to try his two friends.

The King called together the soldier and the doctor and ordered them to go out and find the most valuable thing in this world. The two men were to search the world for one year, and after a year they were to return. Then each man was to bring back to the King what he thought was the most valuable thing in this world.

Both men promised the King that they would search hard to find the most valuable thing in this world. So the two men started off together. After a week's journey the men came to a beautiful castle. There they decided to separate, but each man agreed that he would return to the castle just as soon as he had found what he thought to be the most valuable thing in this world.

The soldier was quite certain that he would find the most valuable thing in this world. The soldier crossed the seas; he climbed mountains; he visited big cities and small towns. The soldier found costly rugs, expensive diamonds, and precious pearls. But the soldier bought none of these things. The soldier knew that his friend, the King, already had all these things. The soldier was looking for something different, something very special. He was looking for something that the King did not own. He was looking for the most valuable thing in this world.

After visiting several countries, the soldier finally went to Africa and there he found a most unusual gift. It was an expensive gift, but it was something that the King could use, something that the King did not own. It was a long magic tube made of ivory, and the magic tube looked very much like a piece of pipe. You may think that the long magic tube was a strange gift. Well, it was a strange gift. When a person looked through the magic tube, he could see anybody in any part of the world. The King could look through the magic tube at any time and see just what his people were doing. That's why the soldier bought the magic tube even though it cost him several hundred dollars. The soldier knew that the magic tube would please the King. The soldier felt that the magic tube was the most valuable thing in this world.

Now, what about the doctor? Well, the doctor, too, visited many countries in his search for the most valuable thing in this world. The doctor looked at many gifts but none satisfied him. He, too, wanted to find something unusual, something that the King did not already own. The doctor spent many sleepless nights and tiresome days wondering what he could buy.

It's a good thing that the doctor didn't become discouraged, because in India the doctor found something unusual. It was the only one that could be found in this world. It was something that would certainly please the King. What did the doctor find in India? The doctor found a magic apple, one smell of which would cure anyone of any sickness. The doctor knew that the magic apple was very valuable and very precious. So the doctor bought the magic apple for the King. I don't have to tell you that the doctor was happy. The doctor thought that his gift was the most valuable thing in this world.

After several weeks the soldier and the doctor returned to the beautiful castle and each man began to boast about his gift. Each man showed his gift and each man felt that his gift was the most valuable thing in this world.

"Let's see what the King is doing!" said the soldier as he held up and looked through his magic tube.

What the soldier saw made him tremble and shake. The soldier saw the King stretched on a bed. The King was sick. The King was very sick.

When the doctor heard the terrible news, his eyes

flashed. "Let's hurry to the King!" he said excitedly. "My magic apple will cure him."

Well, the two men lost no time. They ran most of the way home, and when they reached the side of the King, the King didn't know them. The King wasn't able to speak. The doctor said nothing, but he held the magic apple close to the King's face. One smell of the magic apple was enough. The King opened his eyes, smiled, and began to speak. The King was cured! The King was well again!

Now I suppose you are wondering which gift was the more valuable. Children, both gifts were valuable. Both gifts were necessary to save the life of the King.

I think that the King in our story was very lucky to have had two friends like the soldier and the doctor. It was a good thing, too, that the soldier and the doctor bought those valuable gifts? Do you know, children, that you, too, are very fortunate? Very often your souls get sick. Your souls become sick whenever you commit sin. If you do two things, however, your souls can be cured. Both things are absolutely necessary.

First of all, you must examine your conscience. You must look into your soul and find out just what sins are there. When you examine your conscience, it's just like looking through a magic tube to see what sins are on your soul. Then, after you have found out what sins are there, you must use the great gift given you by Jesus, the Sacrament of

Penance. In other words, after you have found out what your sins are, you must go to confession. No matter how many sins are on your soul, if you are sorry for them, the Sacrament of Penance will remove all of them. Then your soul will be cured. The sins will be gone and God's grace will come into your soul.

You can see, then, that the examination of conscience and the Sacrament of Penance are very important. Both are absolutely necessary when you want the terrible disease of sin to be removed from your souls. Children, think about your sins often, and go often to confession!

God bless you and take good care of yourself!

21. The Wooden Pony

RANDY was a black and white pony. Now Randy wasn't a real, live, honest-to-goodness pony. Oh, no! Randy was a wooden pony that jumped and galloped on a noisy old merry-go-round. Little children loved Randy because he was so small, and they liked to ride the black and white pony.

At first, Randy enjoyed carrying excited children on his back and he liked the music of the merry-go-round. But after a while, Randy tired of life because every day was the same for him. Every day he went up and down, around and around in a circle, but he went nowhere. The little pony longed to get away from the noise of the busy old merry-go-round. He longed to get away from the watchful eye of his father who pranced and galloped right by his side. Yes, Randy wanted to run away. But Randy couldn't run away because he was fastened tightly to the noisy old merry-go-round. So there was nothing that the little pony could do except prance and gallop and run around in a circle. It was a hard life for a little pony even though Randy was only a make-

believe pony, a little black and white wooden pony.

Well, one day last summer little Randy worked very hard. Some children had a picnic in the park, and Randy spent most of the day carrying a child on his back. That night the little pony was dizzy and he ached with pain. Randy was never so tired in all his life. In fact, Randy was so tired, that just as soon as the merry-go-round stopped, the little fellow fell asleep right on his feet.

Now, I never knew that wooden ponies dream, but that night little Randy had a dream. Randy dreamt that he was a real live pony, a real black and white pony. And what do you think? In his dream Randy decided to run away from his father. So, run away the pony did. At first, he was very happy. He was free and he could do as he pleased. Randy was certainly excited.

But little ponies, you know, get hungry just like little children. So Randy stopped in an orchard to eat some apples, but an angry old farmer chased the pony away. When Randy stopped in a field to eat hay, a boy tried to lasso him with a rope. When the pony stopped at a brook to drink water, an ugly old bee stung him hard. Little Randy began to realize then that being a real live pony wasn't too much fun. Randy wished that he were back home with his father. He wanted to be just a little wooden pony prancing and galloping by his father's side on a noisy old merry-go-round.

Randy was very sad, until, all of a sudden, he heard music. He raised his ears and listened. Sure enough, it was real music, band music, and the little fellow dashed off in the direction of the music. He crossed several fields and every minute the music became louder and louder. Finally, the little fellow stopped and smiled. Why, the music was coming from a circus band, and little Randy had never seen a circus.

Randy walked slowly toward the circus tent and, as he drew near, he could hardly believe his eyes. Outside the tent stood ten or twelve black and white ponies. Randy wondered whether the circus ponies would be friendly. Anyway, he decided to take a chance. Randy joined the group but the other ponies paid no attention to him. Randy even tried to rub noses with the strangers, but the circus ponies moved away. That hurt little Randy, but just then a man dressed in white and carrying a long whip blew a whistle, and ordered the ponies to go inside the tent. Randy tried to run away, but when the circus man raised his whip, Randy followed the other ponies into the tent.

Randy knew that the circus man had made a mistake and he knew that it was time for the circus ponies to do their act. Randy was nervous and afraid because he knew that he couldn't do any tricks. For a moment, he thought about the merry-go-round and wished he were home. Oh, if he were only back home by his father's side!

The circus band played and the people clapped and cheered when the black and white ponies entered the center ring. Randy knew that he didn't belong in the ring and he was the last pony to enter. First, the ponies bowed to the crowd and Randy tried to bow, too. Of course, that was easy, but Randy wondered what the ponies would do next. When the circus man blew his whistle, the ponies walked around the ring and Randy followed them. Then the ponies began to trot and Randy trotted, too. Then the ponies began to run. Faster and faster the ponies flew around the ring almost too fast for little Randy. Around and around and around they went until Randy, tired and dizzy, suddenly stumbled and the little fellow fell to the ground with a terrific crash. And when Randy awoke, he was still going around in a circle. Randy wasn't going around in a circle at the circus; he was going around in a circle on a noisy old merry-go-round.

When Randy realized that he had been dreaming, he was very happy. He was happy to be home. He was happy because he was close to his father. Never again would the little fellow want to run away, not even in a dream. Randy knew then that the best place for a little wooden pony was close to his father prancing and galloping on a noisy old merry-go-round.

Children, sometimes you run away from God, your Father. And when you run away from God, you get into trouble and fall into sin. Like the wooden pony, don't think you can be happy away from your Father! You can't be happy when you are away from God. You can't be happy when you fall into sin.

Boys and girls, the best place for you is close to God, your Father. Don't ever make the mistake of thinking that you don't need God! If, however, you make the mistake of running away from God and falling into sin, go back to God as soon as possible! Go to confession! God will always forgive you. God will always take you back.

God bless you and take good care of yourself!

22. The Devil Makes a Discovery

THEY say that the devil has many helpers. These helpers are little devils who try to lead people into sin. Little devils are always busy. They never sleep. They work night and day and they never get tired. Little devils know all the tricks of the big devil and they work hard to get souls away from God. Little devils win many souls for their boss in hell, and that's what the devil wants.

Well, one day each of the little devils received a bright red envelope. When each little devil saw his bright red envelope, he shook with fear because he knew that his mail came from hell. No wonder the little devils were afraid to open their envelopes!

There was a letter in each envelope and each letter was the same. Each letter was written by the big boss himself. I suppose you are wondering what the devil wrote to his little helpers. Well, the devil wanted more children in hell. So he ordered his little helpers to get busy and work hard on little children.

Did the little devils get busy? You bet they did!

The little devils told bad stories to children and showed them dirty pictures. They bothered little children when they tried to pray. They told boys and girls to stay in bed on Sunday mornings and not to go to Mass. They tried to keep children from receiving Holy Communion. Why, they even tried to get boys and girls to eat meat on Friday. Yes, the little devils tried hard to lead little children into sin and to get more of them into hell.

But do you know that the little devils didn't get very far? No, sir! The little devils couldn't get children to fall into sin. In fact, boys and girls wouldn't listen to them. The children were smart and they weren't fooled by a lot of little devils.

Well, the big devil in hell tried to be patient. He waited and waited for children to come to him, but the children didn't come. Then one day the devil became very angry and flew into a rage.

"Something is wrong!" yelled the devil at the top of his voice. "I'll go after the children myself. I'll get some children down here in hell."

So the devil himself left hell and came to earth. Of course, nobody saw the devil but he was here just the same. The devil followed boys and girls for several days. He followed them into their homes and into their schools. He was even bold enough to follow children into church. The devil tempted several children and tried to lead them into sin, but the children paid no attention.

The devil was certainly puzzled. He was disgusted. He knew that something was wrong and he was determined to find out what it was. The devil thought for a long time and then, what do you suppose he decided to do? The devil decided to follow the Sheridan children for a whole day and see what they would do. Maybe the Sheridan children would show him what was wrong and why children were not going to hell.

The next morning the devil was on the job bright and early and he hurried over to the Sheridan home. The devil saw Jack, Lynn, and Anne Sheridan get out of bed. He saw them when they said their prayers and he followed them to breakfast. Why, the devil even went to school with the Sheridan children although they didn't know it. He watched the three children when they played after school, and he was right in the dining room when they ate their supper.

After supper the whole Sheridan family knelt down in the living room. Little Jack Sheridan said the Rosary and the rest of the family answered the prayers.

This was too much for the devil. "The Rosary is keeping children out of hell," said the devil in a sad voice for he knew he was beaten. It's a wonder that the Sheridans didn't hear him.

The devil left the Sheridan home in a hurry. Then he went to other homes and, sure enough, the devil saw other families saying the Rosary. The next day the devil went to some schools and saw large groups of children saying the Rosary together. He saw boys and girls saying the Rosary in church. Now the devil was sure of what was wrong. Children were saying the Rosary and he knew that as long as children prayed to Mary, he couldn't get them into hell.

The devil threw up his arms in disgust. He knew that he didn't have a chance. He was licked by the Rosary. So the beaten old devil hung his head in shame and hurried back to hell.

Boys and girls, you should say the Rosary every day. That's the way to tell Mary that you want her to protect you from the devil. Mary wants your soul for Jesus, and don't forget that the devil wants your soul, too. If you say the Rosary every day, you can be pretty sure that the devil will keep away from you. When the Sheridan children said the Rosary, the devil couldn't stay near them. If you say the Rosary, the devil will keep away from you. The devil hates the Rosary and he hates boys and girls who say the Rosary. So, if you want to be safe from the devil, say the Rosary every day!

Don't get the idea that it takes a long time to say the Rosary! Why, you can say the Rosary in about twelve minutes. Twelve minutes a day spent with Mary will keep the devil away. That's worth knowing. Isn't it?

God bless you and take good care of yourself!

23. The Dime in the Left Shoe

BOBBY MURRAY collected things. He was always saving something. Bobby saved old stamps and he had a very large collection. He saved small crosses, odd buttons, and old coins. Now I don't know how much these things were worth, but there was one thing that Bobby owned that he thought was very precious. It was a ten-cent piece, a dime that was dated 1900. That coin was Bobby's greatest treasure and the boy called it his "lucky dime."

Whenever Bobby went fishing, he always carried his lucky dime in one of his pockets. Of course, others caught fish, but it seems that Bobby always caught more fish than any of his friends. Bobby always felt that his lucky dime helped him to catch more fish.

Examinations never bothered Bobby. Just before an examination he would squeeze his lucky coin, and Bobby always got good marks. His friends used to laugh at him, but Bobby had great faith in that lucky dime.

Bobby liked to go to a picnic because there were always races at a picnic. Sure enough, Bobby always won some of the prizes. Bobby felt that his lucky dime helped him to win.

Bobby Murray carried that dime in his pocket for several years. When the boy thought that he needed help, he would slip his hand into his pocket and pinch his dime. When Bobby played basketball on the high school team, he always slipped his dime into his left shoe. Bobby, you know, was a very good basketball player and he scored a great many points for his team. When his friends praised him, Bobby just smiled and told no one his secret. I think that Bobby was really afraid to play basketball without his lucky dime.

Bobby played football, too. Yes, he was a member of the high school team and he played very well. Let me tell you about the first game of the season! Bobby's team played very hard in that first game because they wanted to win. In one of the plays the quarterback threw the ball to Bobby. Bobby caught the ball and started to run. The boy ran only a short distance when he was tackled, and just about all the boys on both teams piled on top of Bobby. When both teams were ready for the next play, Bobby was still on the ground. He tried to get up but he couldn't move.

The trainer ran out to help Bobby. He looked at the boy's leg and shook his head. Well, Bobby didn't play any more football that day. He was taken to the hospital and the doctors found that Bobby had broken his leg. And what do you think? When a nurse took off Bobby's shoes, she found Bobby's lucky dime in his left shoe.

That was one time when Bobby's lucky dime was no good. Bobby's lucky dime didn't keep him from breaking his leg. Bobby thought that dime would always bring him good luck, but Bobby was wrong. That dime never brought Bobby good luck. He was wrong to think that a dime could do wonderful things for him. Bobby Murray was just a foolish boy, a silly boy to believe such nonsense. God never helps anyone who thinks he has a lucky dime. God doesn't work that way. God never promised to help or protect anyone who puts a dime in his left shoe. Such nonsense makes God laugh.

Now don't get the idea that a Catholic medal is like a lucky dime! When you wear a Catholic medal or carry one in your pocket, you don't look on it as a good-luck piece. That medal won't keep you from having an accident, and that medal won't save you from drowning. Oh, no!

Isn't it true that many of you carry a picture of your mother in your wallet or purse? And isn't it true that every time you look at the picture of your mother, you think about your mother? Well, that's the same reason why you wear or carry a Catholic medal. Every time you look at your medal you think about Jesus, or His Mother, or some saint. Very often when you look at your medal, you pray to Jesus, or Mary, or some saint. In other words, your medal is just a reminder. Your medal reminds you to pray to Jesus, Mary, and the saints. Your medal is not a good-luck piece.

Don't forget that Jesus, Mary, and the saints in heaven know what is going on down here on earth. They know the boys and girls who are wearing their medals. They know the ones who are honoring them. When you wear or carry a medal, your friends in heaven keep a special eye on you.

Children, don't get any wrong ideas about your Catholic medal! Your medal is not a charm. Wear a medal, yes, and when you look at the picture on your medal, say a prayer to the saint whose picture is there! The more you pray to the saint, the more he will help you. A medal will help you to love the saints more, but you will never get anything from having an old dime in your left shoe.

God bless you and take good care of yourself!

24. Half Past Three

HALF past three! That's a magic moment for boys and girls. At half past three the school bell rings and children close their books because school is over for another day. At half past three it's time for play, time for baseball or football, time for flying kites, time to play marbles and other games. Yes, when it's half past three, it's time for fun.

Stevie McGill, like all boys, liked to play and have fun. Stevie was always happy at half past three. He was always one of the first boys to leave school, but he didn't go at once to the playground. Nor did the little fellow go straight home. Oh, no! When school was out, where do you think Stevie went? He went first to the church. The boy didn't stay in church very long, just for a few minutes. Then Stevie left the church and joined his friends at the playground.

I suppose Stevie McGill thought that no one was watching him. But someone did watch him. Every day at half past three Father Grace watched Stevie from the window of his home and the priest wondered. He wondered why the boy went to the church

every day. He wondered what the boy did in the
church. The priest knew that Stevie didn't stay in
church very long and, therefore, he couldn't say
many prayers. Father Grace was certainly puzzled.

Well, one day Father Grace decided to find out
about Stevie's visits. So a little before half past three,
the priest went to the church, hid in the vestry, and
waited for Stevie. Sure enough, a little after half
past three, the church door opened and Stevie McGill
hurried down the aisle. The priest saw Stevie kneel
before the altar, but Stevie couldn't see the priest.
Father Grace watched the boy and waited, but the
priest didn't have to wait very long.

Stevie blessed himself and looked right up at the
altar. "I'm Stevie McGill," said the boy out loud,
"and I'm back with my troubles. My mother is sick

again and I wish You'd make her better. My dog got into another fight this noon and this time he got licked. Can't You make Boots be a good dog? And there's one more thing — please help me with my arithmetic, because that's hard for me! Thanks, Jesus, for everything! That's all this time. I've got to go now."

As Stevie McGill hurried out of the church, Father Grace smiled, and I'm sure that God smiled, too. God smiled because He knew that Stevie's prayer was a real prayer — it came right from the boy's heart. Stevie was honest and he was sincere. The boy told God just what was bothering him. He told God what he wanted, and he asked God to help him. And another thing! Stevie didn't forget to thank God. The boy didn't use any fancy words and he didn't read out of a book. He talked to God just like any boy would talk to a friend, and I'm pretty sure that God understood the little fellow. I'll bet that Stevie's prayer was one of the best prayers that God heard that day.

Children, it is not hard to pray, it's easy to pray. When you pray, all that you have to do is talk to God. Thank God for the things He has given you and ask God for the things you need! Like Stevie, you can use your own words and God will understand. You don't need a book, either, because the best prayers come right out of your heart. Your prayers don't have to be long because very often the short prayers are the best prayers. When you pray, you know, you show God that you are thinking about Him and that's what God wants. God doesn't want you to forget Him, and you won't forget God if you pray.

Don't forget that God is everywhere! When you pray, you don't even have to go to church. You can pray in school. You can pray on the street. You can pray on the playground. If you take only a moment and say "hello" to God, that's a prayer. No matter when or where you pray, God will be listening.

Isn't it true that you don't say enough prayers? You could say more prayers. Well, then, let's try to say more prayers! Try to say a good many prayers today! Try again tomorrow and try every day! Make every day a day of prayer! That's the best way to keep close to God.

I really think that Stevie McGill taught us a lesson this morning. That little fellow taught us how to pray. I think, too, that this world would be a much better world if we had a few more boys and girls like Stevie McGill. Don't you think so? Well, I do!

God bless you and take good care of yourself!

25. The Empty Shoes

IF I were to ask you which night is the most exciting night of the whole year, I know what your answer would be. You would tell me that Christmas eve is the best. Yes, that's true! The night before Christmas is certainly a great night. That's the night when children hang up their stockings. That's the night when children wonder and hope. They wonder what Santa Claus will bring. They hope that Santa will leave a lot of presents. The night before Christmas is a night of dreams — about sleds and trains and cowboy suits. Christmas eve is the night when the whole world is happy, a night that is dear to all boys and girls.

Do you know what the children of Spain do on Christmas eve? Well, the children of Spain don't hang up their stockings. Instead, they put their shoes on the sill outside their bedroom windows, and during the night the Three Kings go about putting gifts into every little shoe they find waiting for them. So, on Christmas morning the children of Spain don't find their gifts in their stockings: they find their gifts in their shoes.

Now it was Christmas eve in Spain and the seven-year-old Prince was very excited. Like all the other children, the Prince wondered what the Three Kings would bring. While the Prince had all kinds of toys, he wanted more toys. Why, he even wrote a letter to the Three Kings and asked them for many gifts. The Prince put his letter in one of his shoes and placed the shoes outside his bedroom window. The boy was sure that Christmas morning would be a happy one.

Christmas morning came early for the little Prince. It came very, very early. In fact, the Prince was the first one awake on Christmas morning. He jumped out of bed, ran across the room, and raised the window. And what do you think? The little Prince found no presents, no toys, no gifts. The Three Kings had been at the boy's window all right, because the letter was gone, but the shoes were empty.

The Prince stood at the window and tears trickled down his cheeks. He was heartbroken. Disappointed. Sad. The boy could hardly believe that his shoes were empty. He couldn't understand why he hadn't received any presents. At that moment the young Prince was just about the saddest little boy in all Spain.

The boy ran to his mother and awakened her. He cried again as he told his mother about the empty shoes. Of course, the mother was surprised, too, but she listened and wondered. The mother thought hard for a long time and finally she began to speak.

"Son," said the mother kindly, "I think I know why your shoes are empty. The Three Kings knew that you didn't need any toys, so they gave your toys to poor children. I think, too, that the Three Kings wanted to teach you a lesson and that lesson is this — you can't always have what you want."

The boy's mother was right, but her words didn't help the Prince very much. The Prince thought about all the other boys who were happy that morning. He thought about the other boys who found toys in their shoes. He wondered why he couldn't be like other boys. Oh, it was hard for the Prince to understand.

Now I suppose you think that the Prince had a very sad Christmas. Well, he did have a very sad morning until just before breakfast. The boy was about to sit down at the table when his mother told him that someone wanted to see him at the back door. The Prince hurried to the door, opened it, and was he surprised! There, standing in the yard and tied to a tree, was a beautiful black and white pony. Yes, the pony was for the little Prince. A Christmas present for the boy! The little fellow clapped his hands and shouted with delight. He forgot all about the empty shoes and now he was really happy. The Prince asked for toys and received a beautiful pony. The boy couldn't have what he wanted, but he received something better.

Children, when you kneel down to pray, just keep in mind that you can't always have what you want.

You may pray for something that you think you just have to have to make you happy, but God always knows best. God knows what you need, and very often God may not give you the thing for which you pray. God may give you something else, something that you never ask for in your prayers, something much better than the thing for which you pray. Don't ever get the idea that God doesn't answer your prayers! God hears every prayer and He answers every prayer. God may not answer your prayers the way you want them to be answered, but He will answer them just the same. God will always give you what is best for you.

Children, pray, and pray often! Remember, however, you can't always have what you want. God will answer every prayer, and God's answer will always be the best answer.

God bless you and take good care of yourself!

26. The Boy Who Almost Lost Thanksgiving Day

JIMMY MAHR liked cranberries, and he liked turkey, too. Cranberries and turkey were on the top of Jimmy's list of good things to eat.

It was the Sunday before Thanksgiving, and seven-year-old Jimmy was wondering. The little fellow was wondering about the great day that was coming soon. He wondered whether he would have cranberries and turkey for his Thanksgiving dinner.

"Are we going to have cranberries and turkey for Thanksgiving?" Jimmy finally asked his father.

The father waited for a moment and then shook his head. "Jimmy," said the father, "we're not going to celebrate Thanksgiving this year."

Little Jimmy was puzzled. "Does that mean that we're not going to have cranberries and turkey?" he asked.

"That's right!" answered the father. "No cranberries and no turkey!"

Jimmy couldn't understand. "Why aren't we going

to have cranberries and turkey?" he asked and there were tears in his eyes.

The boy's father looked very serious. "Jimmy," he said, "Thanksgiving is a day for people who want to thank Jesus for all the good things they have received from Him. Jesus, you know, has been very good to you, but I've never once heard you thank Jesus. When you say your prayers at night, you are always asking for something. You ought to do something about that!"

When the father left the room, little Jimmy sat down on the floor and began to think. He thought about what his father had said. Yes, his father was right. He had never thanked Jesus for anything. Well, the little fellow thought and thought, and he wondered what he could do to show Jesus that he was thankful.

All of a sudden, Jimmy got an idea. "I know what I'll do," he said to himself. "I'll give Jesus something. I'll give Jesus the best thing I own."

Jimmy ran upstairs to his playroom and looked at his toys. He looked at his drum, his electric train, his skates, his football, and his marbles. No, those things weren't good enough for Jesus, but Jimmy saw two things on the floor that he thought Jesus would like. He picked up both of them and set them aside. Then the boy wrote something on a piece of paper.

Pretty soon, little Jimmy Mahr tiptoed down the stairs with a bundle under his arm. The boy opened the door very quietly and hurried down the street. Where did Jimmy go? He hurried to the nearby church. There were no people in the church at the time, and that's just what Jimmy wanted. The boy tiptoed down the long aisle of the church right up to the altar steps. There on the top step of the altar Jimmy Mahr left his little bundle. Then Jimmy left the church.

When Father McCarthy came into the church the next morning, he was more than surprised to find a bundle laying on the top step of the altar. At first, the priest was afraid to open the bundle. He felt the bundle very carefully, shook it, and wondered. Then the priest opened the package and what do you think he found inside? A pair of cowboy boots! And that isn't all! In one of the boots the priest found a letter. Father McCarthy smiled when he read the letter, and you'll smile, too. Here's what the letter said:

"Dear Jesus:

"Thank You for everything You have given me! Now I want to give You something nice. Here are my cowboy boots! I hope they'll fit You.

"Jimmy Mahr."

Well, after Mass, even before he had his breakfast, Father McCarthy called Jimmy Mahr's father on the telephone, and, when Mr. Mahr heard what his boy had done, he smiled. Mr. Mahr was pleased that his boy had learned a lesson. Jimmy Mahr had learned to say "thanks."

Now I suppose you are wondering about Jimmy

Mahr's Thanksgiving dinner. Well, the Mahr family had a grand feast on that day with plenty of good things to eat. But do you know what Jimmy Mahr ate most for dinner? Cranberries and turkey! Cranberries and turkey!

Boys and girls, there are too many children like Jimmy Mahr. Yes, there are too many boys and girls who are always asking Jesus for something and they never thank Him. Some boys and girls never thank Jesus for being good to them and I hope you're not one of them. When you pray, ask Jesus for the things you need, but don't forget to say prayers of thanks, too! Prayers of thanks are mighty important because they tell Jesus that you are grateful.

No one likes a person who is not grateful and Jesus doesn't like a person who never says "thanks." If you don't thank Jesus for His gifts, maybe Jesus won't be so generous with you. You wouldn't want that to happen, would you?

I don't think boys and girls mean to be ungrateful, but they certainly act that way. They forget to thank Jesus. Don't you forget to thank Him! Now, if you want to show Jesus that you are grateful, you won't have to give Him your cowboy boots. Jesus doesn't want your cowboy boots. He doesn't need your cowboy boots. How can you show Jesus that you are grateful? Just by saying prayers of thanks!

God bless you and take good care of yourself!

27. The Tired Old Clock

SEVENTY-THREE years! That's a long, long time. It's a long time to live. It's a long time to work. Very few people, you know, live for seventy-three years, and I've never heard of any person who worked seventy-three years.

Now, in the little village of Fair View there was a grand old clock that was seventy-three years old. For seventy-three years the faithful old clock lived in the steeple of the village church. Day and night the old clock smiled down on its many friends. The clock was never fast. It was never late. It was always on time. And every hour the grand old clock struck out the time of day or night. The town clock suffered in the summer heat: it shivered in the cold of winter. For seventy-three years the village clock was everyone's friend. I've often wondered how many people have looked up at that clock. I've often wondered how many people have set their watches by the town clock. I suppose I'll never know.

The people of Fair View loved their village clock, but there was one thing that the people didn't know. The old clock was tired. It was very tired. The old clock was tired of working twenty-four hours a day. It was tired of ticking and tocking day after day and year after year. Why wouldn't it be tired? Hadn't the old clock worked hard for seventy-three years? The old clock needed a rest, but no one knew it.

Well, one night last January it was very cold. It was very quiet, too, because the people of the village had gone to bed. As the tired old clock looked down upon the darkened village, it decided to do something that it had never done before.

"Now that everyone is asleep," said the clock to itself, "I think I'll take a little nap. A little sleep will be good for me."

So the tired old clock stopped its ticking and tocking and went to sleep. But what do you think? The old clock was so tired that it forgot to wake up. And was there excitement in the little village of Fair View the next morning? Yes, there was plenty of excitement, and that sleeping old clock caused lots of trouble. The morning train arrived to carry men and women to the city, but there were no passengers. Breakfasts were late, the paper boy was late, and people were late for work. Many people didn't go to work at all. Why, the priest was even late for Mass and children were late for school. Everyone was angry and everyone blamed the tired old clock that went to sleep.

Can't you see how much the people of Fair View depended upon the village clock? That clock steered the lives of every person in that village. That clock got the people to work on time. That clock got children to school on time. That clock brought people together for business, for pleasure, and for work. That clock told people when they should go to parties or the movie. It told people when they should go to bed. The old town clock did a grand job for seventy-three years, but the old clock failed one night last January when it got tired and went to sleep.

Do you know, boys and girls, that God has given each of you something that steers your lives? God has given each of you something that never wears out, something that never gets tired, something that never goes to sleep. This gift from God is called your conscience. Your conscience is the little voice inside of you that always checks you, the voice that always tells you what is right and what is wrong, the voice that is trying to lead you to heaven.

Let's suppose that you are walking down the street and you see a large basket of apples in front of a store. You wish you had one of the apples. You are just about to steal an apple when a voice inside of you tells you not to steal. That voice is your conscience. Your conscience reminds you that it's a sin to steal. So you change your mind and don't steal the apple. That's the way your conscience works. It's always on the job to tell you what is right and what is wrong. Your conscience pulls you away from sin and leads you to God.

Did you ever fall into sin? Did you ever disobey God or break one of His laws? How did you feel after you committed the sin? Were you happy? Indeed, you were not! You felt guilty. Do you know why you felt guilty? Your conscience was telling you that you had done wrong. Your conscience was warning you not to do that thing again. Your conscience spoke to you and checked you and warned you about the future.

There is one big mistake that too many children make. They don't listen to their conscience and that's when they get into trouble. When children don't listen to their conscience, they usually fall into sin. Of course, your conscience will bother and annoy you and it's a good thing that it does. After all, most boys and girls want to be good. No one wants to be bad. So, when your conscience bothers you, your conscience is really helping you. Your conscience is the voice of God. When your conscience nudges you or whispers to you, God is warning you to be careful. God is telling you to keep away from sin.

Children, God doesn't want to lose you. That's why He has given you a conscience. So, when your conscience speaks, listen! Then follow your conscience in all things! Your conscience will keep you close to God. Your conscience will lead you to God.

God bless you and take good care of yourself!

28. How To Be a Cowboy

LITTLE Tommy Herrmann liked cowboys. He liked to read about cowboys and he never missed a cowboy movie. Tommy even had a cowboy suit and loved to play cowboy with his little friends. Tommy loved all cowboys and every cowboy was Tommy's hero. But there was one cowboy whom Tommy loved best of all. That cowboy was Bob Curwood.

One day while watching a cowboy picture on TV, Tommy got an idea. "Gee!" he said to himself, "I wish I were a cowboy." Then the little fellow began to think. He wondered how he could become a cowboy. Well, the little fellow thought and thought, and finally, Tommy decided to do something.

Tommy didn't tell anybody, but do you know what the little boy did? Tommy wrote a letter. He wrote a letter to his famous friend, Bob Curwood, and here's what Tommy said in his letter:

"Dear Bob Curwood,

"How old do I have to be to be a cowboy? Please tell me what I have to do and where I can go to learn to be a cowboy.

"Your sincere friend,
"Tommy Herrmann."

Now I don't know what Bob Curwood did when he read Tommy's letter, but I am pretty sure that Bob Curwood must have smiled. Yes, and Bob Curwood did something more than smile. Bob Curwood answered Tommy's letter. Yes, sir! Bob Curwood wrote a letter to little Tommy and here's what the famous cowboy said in his letter:

"Dear Tommy,

"You asked me where you could go to learn to be a cowboy. When you get a little older, maybe you won't want to be a cowboy. There are lots of other ways of being happy, and the only place where a cowboy's life is always happy is in the movies.

"Now if you really want to be a cowboy, go about it this way. First of all, take lots of exercise by playing games with other good boys! Be kind to your parents and obey them! Secondly, don't be mean! Be pure in your thoughts, words, and actions! Be honest and hate lies! Remember, if you conquer yourself, you will learn how to conquer wild cattle. Be sure to pray and go to church because a cowboy may be killed any time and he should be ready to die. Finally, when you are a cowboy, you won't have time to study, so study now! Go to school every day and study hard! Obey your teachers and like them! And don't forget to talk over this cowboy business with your father and mother! If God wants you to be a cowboy, you'll come out right in the end. Ask God to help you!

> "Your friend,
> "Bob Curwood."

I don't have to tell you that little Tommy Herrmann was pleased with his letter from Bob Curwood. That letter is something very precious, and that letter means a great deal to the little fellow. And what do you think? Tommy is trying to do everything that Bob Curwood told him to do. Yes, Tommy is very serious about this cowboy business. He is following Bob Curwood's advice because Tommy Herrmann wants to be a cowboy.

Now I don't know whether little Tommy will ever be a cowboy, but I do know this. If Tommy follows the advice given by his friend, Tommy will grow up to be a very fine man. Bob Curwood's advice is good for everyone of you children, too, whether you are going to be a doctor, or a fireman, or a nurse, or a teacher, or a cowboy. If you follow Bob Curwood's advice, you'll come out on top. You can't miss.

Are you going to be a cowboy? Maybe you are, and maybe you are not. Well, no matter what you are going to be, start now and play with good boys and girls! Be kind and obey! Be clean and be honest! Go to church and say your prayers! Go to school and study hard! Obey your teachers and parents! Ask God's help in everything you do! That's the way to be a good nurse, a good lawyer, a good policeman, a good priest, or a good cowboy.

Children, it's not too early to start getting ready. God alone knows what you are going to be when you grow up. Maybe God wants you to be a cowboy. Maybe He wants you to be a priest, or a fireman. Maybe God wants you to make automobiles, or be a plumber. Well, whatever God wants you to do, you will want to do it well. The thing that you should do now and should do often is pray. Pray and ask God to tell you what He wants you to do. Ask God to help you like what He wants you to do. Ask God to lead you in the right way. After all, you want to do God's will. So, even though it will be a long time before you are a priest or a cowboy, get ready now by asking God to help you. You don't want to make any mistakes.

Bob Curwood gave little Tommy some very good advice. It's good advice for you, too. Pray now, and pray every day so that you will be good priests, good teachers, good nurses, good policemen, yes, and even good cowboys!

God bless you and take good care of yourself!

Index of Topics